Starry Night

ROBIN JONES GUNN

BETHANY HOUSE PUBLISHERS
MINNEAPOLIS, MINNESOTA 55438

Starry Night
Revised edition 1999
Copyright © 1993, 1999
Robin Jones Gunn

Edited by Janet Kobobel Grant
Cover illustration and design by Lookout Design Group

Focus on the Family books are available at special quantity discounts when purchased in bulk by corporations, organizations, churches, or groups. Special imprints, messages, and excerpts can be produced to meet your needs. For more information, contact: Resource Sales Group, Focus on the Family, 8605 Explorer Drive, Colorado Springs, CO 80920; or phone (800) 932-9123.

A Focus on the Family book published by
Bethany House Publishers
11400 Hampshire Avenue South
Bloomington, Minnesota 55438
www.bethanyhouse.com

Bethany House Publishers is a Division of
Baker Book House Company, Grand Rapids, Michigan.

Printed in the United States of America

Library of Congress Cataloging-in-Publication Data

Gunn, Robin Jones, 1955–
    Starry night / Robin Jones Gunn
       p. cm. — (The Christy Miller Series ; 8)
    Summary: While visiting her college friends and later spending Christmas vacation with her family instead of her friends, 16-year-old Christy is reminded of the restrictions placed on her activities by her parents.
    ISBN 1–56179–721–9
    [1. Christian life—Fiction. 2. Parent and child—Fiction.] I. Series:
Gunn, Robin Jones, 1955–   Christy Miller Series ; 8.
PZ7.G972St   1993
[Fic]—dc20
                                      92–15030
                                         CIP
                                         AC

03 04 05 06 07 08 09 / 16 15 14 13 12 11 10 9 8 7 6 5

To my sister, Julie Ann Jones Johnson,
who has stood by my heart many times as
I've counted stars.
With special appreciation to Rich
Mullins, Margaret Becker, and Bryan Duncan, who
have each brilliantly put to music the starry-night
thoughts I've attempted to write in this story.

Contents

1. Car Trek: The Next Generation   1
2. Chocolate-Chip Rescue 10
3. Opposites Don't Attract, Do They? 21
4. I'm Not Dreaming of a White Christmas 35
5. Camera-Shy Christy 44
6. Thanks a Lot, Uncle Doug! 52
7. Snow Wars 61
8. Diamonds in the Sky 72
9. Spin Dry 81
10. Just Friends 92
11. The White Rose Parade 101
12. Katie, You Didn't! 112
13. Marti's Party 125
14. Counting Stars 135

CHAPTER ONE

Car Trek: The Next Generation

"Don't laugh," 16-year-old Katie said to her best friend, Christy Miller. "Just keep driving, and don't laugh."

"I'm not laughing," Christy said, pressing her foot on the brake pedal as she turned into the mall parking lot. "Honest. I'm not laughing."

Christy brushed back her nutmeg-brown hair and glanced at Katie out of the corner of her eye. "Is it okay if I park behind the pet store?"

"That's fine. Do you think anyone will see us? I mean anyone we know?" Katie asked, her bright green eyes scanning the parking lot.

"Probably not," Christy said, aware that her voice carried a hint of laughter. She pulled into a parking space and turned off the engine before cautiously clearing her throat and asking, "Are you going to put on the rest of your costume in the car or when you get inside?"

"You've been waiting for this, haven't you?" Katie said briskly. "You're going to crack up any minute. Admit it. Not all of us can have cushy jobs at the pet store like you."

Katie yanked a pair of felt shoes from her duffel bag and slipped

1

them on. The toes curled up, and bells hung from their ends.

"It's a job, all right?" Katie defended, pulling a matching felt hat from the bag and adjusting it so the bell hung down on the right side of her head. She reached for a pair of plastic, pointed ears and secured them in place. "And if you want to know the truth, I'm proud to be one of Santa's elves," she declared.

Christy could barely hold back her laughter at Katie's elf appearance. She quickly tilted the rearview mirror toward herself. "I think I have something in my eye," she said, trying to quench the laughter bubble in her throat.

One peek in the mirror at her sparkling blue-green eyes warned Christy that the laughter bubble had sprung a leak and was escaping as tiny tears.

She quickly dabbed them away and tried to maintain control for the sake of Katie's self-image.

"Let me see that," Katie said, turning the mirror in her direction and bobbing her head to get a full view of her green hat and pointed elf ears.

She turned to Christy and said, "What kind of best friend are you? Why didn't you tell me I look like the bride of Spockenstein?"

Both girls burst into uncontrollable laughter.

"Beam me up, Santy!" Katie joked.

Christy could hardly breathe, she was laughing so hard.

Katie reached for a tissue and spouted in her best Scottish accent, "I can't hold her together much longer! Captain, I think she's going to blow!" With that, she put the tissue to her face and faked blowing her nose so hard that one of her elf ears fell off.

"Stop, Katie!" Christy forced the words out over her laughter. "We're going to be late for work."

"Okay, okay," Katie said, calming down. "You're right. This

is my first day, and I'd better not be late to Santa's house."

Christy caught her breath and, positioning the mirror back so she could view herself, did a quick fix on her eye makeup. "Come on, Katie. You're going to be the best elf this mall has ever seen. Are you ready?"

"Ready as I'll ever be." Katie grabbed her bag, stepped out of the car, and then immediately ducked back in. With a muffled shriek, she plunged her head beneath the dashboard.

"Duck!" she yelled. "Get down, quick. Maybe he didn't see me."

"Who?" Christy asked, following Katie's orders and scrunching down in the seat.

Before Katie could answer, Christy heard a gentle tap against her window.

She looked at her friend's terror-stricken face as Katie moaned, "Oh no! Too late!"

Christy turned to see Rick Doyle's smiling face peering in her window.

Quickly sitting up, Christy smiled back and pressed the button to roll down the window. It didn't work because the engine was turned off. Without thinking, she opened her car door and bashed Rick in the knees.

Rick, ever the athlete, absorbed the blow as if she had only tapped him.

"Oh, I'm sorry! Are you okay, Rick?"

"Sure," he said, looking past Christy to the curled-up elf in her passenger seat. "I thought I saw Katie."

"Rick!" Katie said brightly, pulling herself up. Her hat tilted all the way to one side, and she looked pretty silly. "I was just, ah . . . I . . . ah, I lost a contact!"

"Lost contact with your home planet is more like it," Rick teased.

Katie smirked and said, "Har, har. I forgot what a funny guy you are, Rick Doyle."

Katie had never been a fan of Rick's. Even when he was voted "most popular" last year at their high school, Katie had written, "As if!" across his picture in her yearbook.

"Yeah, I'm real funny," Rick said. "Too bad I don't have a pair of green tights and some alien ears so I could be as funny as you."

"I happen to be an elf," Katie stated, gathering her things and pushing open the car door. "And I'm proud of it. I also happen to be late for work, so if you'll please excuse me . . ." Katie slammed her door and hurried into the mall.

"I need to get to work, too," Christy said, looping her small, leather backpack over her shoulder.

Rick held the car door for her, and she slid out. She was only inches from him; they hadn't been this close since they dated a few months ago.

Why is Rick being so friendly all of a sudden? What's he up to? Christy wondered.

"Mind if I walk you to work?" he asked. "Or would that make you feel uncomfortable?"

"No, not at all," Christy said, starting toward the mall with Rick beside her.

Why is he asking if I'm uncomfortable? Why is he looking at me so . . . so tenderly?

"So, what brings you to the mall?" Christy asked, trying to appear casual. "Some Christmas shopping? Only 14 shopping days left, you know." *Oh, brother, Christy, do you know how stupid that sounds?*

"Actually, I was on my way home from college for the

weekend, and I remembered that you work on Fridays. I stopped by to see if you were here."

"Well, here I am!" Christy said, realizing how nervous and ridiculous she sounded. But how was she supposed to interpret Rick's sudden appearance, as if silence and tension hadn't existed between them ever since they'd quit dating?

Rick smiled at her as he held the door open, and she slid past him. She didn't dare look up into his chocolate-brown eyes. She even held her breath so she couldn't smell his familiar aftershave and be whisked back into a swirl of memories. She would be strong. She would resist him.

The pet store was only a few yards away, and Christy walked quickly. It was as if once she hit the doorway she would be in the safe zone, and he couldn't confuse her anymore.

This is crazy! What am I thinking? For weeks I've been telling Katie how much I wish I could sit down and talk with Rick to resolve everything. Yet, now that he's only inches from me, I'm running from him, just like I have since the day we met.

With sudden boldness, Christy turned to Rick and said, "I have to get to work now, but I have a break around 6:00. Can you meet me back here then?"

Rick grinned, but he was visibly surprised at her boldness. "Thanks for the invitation, but I already have plans for the evening. I'd like to get together sometime. To talk."

"I'd like that, too," Christy answered softly.

"Okay." Rick nodded. "That's what we'll do then. We'll get together sometime and talk."

"Is that why you stopped by to see if I was here? Were you thinking we could set up a time to talk?"

"Actually, I told Doug I'd remind you about those cookies you promised to bake for us." Rick stuck his hands in his pockets and looked a little sheepish. "Doug is, well . . . he's a cookie freak, you know. I've even seen him go into Oreo withdrawals."

Christy smiled at his joke. Doug was a great guy. She had hoped that when Rick and Doug became roommates, Doug would have a good influence on Rick. It looked as though maybe he had.

"Doug also wanted me to see if you could come down to our God-Lovers Bible study Sunday night. It's from 6:00 to 9:00. I'll draw you a map if you want to come."

Christy wasn't sure how to interpret the invitation. Was Doug inviting her? Or Rick? She knew her parents wouldn't be in favor of her making the 45-minute drive to San Diego by herself.

"I'm not sure I can come," she said, quickly adding, "but I'd like to! Ever since Doug first mentioned your group, I've wanted to come, but I'm not sure my parents would let me drive down by myself."

Christy hoped Rick would pick up on the hint and offer to take her. It would be the perfect opportunity for them to talk. "Oh, right. Those strict parents of yours. I almost forgot," Rick said. "You could invite Rudolph the red-haired elf to come with you."

Pulling a scrap of paper from his pocket, Rick offered it to Christy. "Here's our number. Doug wanted me to give it to you. He'll be there all weekend. Call him if you decide you can come down. I have to go. I'll see you later."

"And we'll get together and talk sometime, right?" Christy hoped she wasn't appearing too eager.

"Right," Rick said, taking small steps backward, as if being sucked into some great mall vacuum. "We'll do that. We'll get together and talk sometime."

He lifted his right hand like a quarterback winding up for a pass and waved at her over the heads of the Christmas shoppers. Then he was gone.

Christy sighed and headed for her safe haven behind the cash register at the pet store, where Jon, her boss, stood helping a customer. Two more were in line.

"So glad you could join us, Miss Miller," Jon said without looking at her. Then to the customer he said, "That will be $17.53, please."

Christy forced herself to look at the clock and grimaced when she saw she was 15 minutes late. Her boss, Jon, was usually easygoing. He wore his hair in a ponytail and had more than once done nice things for Christy. He did like all his employees to be prompt, though.

"I'm sorry, Jon. Do you want me to do that?"

"Sure," he answered as he stepped back to let Christy accept the $20 bill from the customer. Christy counted back the customer's change. By then three more people had stepped in line.

Christy had a feeling she wouldn't get her usual 6:00 break. Maybe Katie would pop in during hers, and Christy could hear how the elf business was going.

But Katie didn't appear at the pet store until closing time. Her face glowed.

"Congratulate me," she said. "I earned a 10 percent bonus tonight!"

"That's great! How did you do it?"

"They said they'd give me a bonus if we sold a certain number of photo packages," Katie explained. "My job is to get the kids to sit on Santa's lap and smile. Of course, the parents are watching, and when they see their kids laughing and looking so cute, they buy more pictures. We did a record-setting amount of business tonight."

"The world's most successful elf," Christy praised her spunky friend. "And to think I knew her when she was merely a high school student."

"Good for you, Katie," Jon said, pulling down the metal cage door that locked up the shop. "What's your 10 percent bonus based on?"

"Based on?" Katie asked.

"You know, based on," Jon said. "You're going to get 10 percent of what?"

Katie blushed. "I don't know. I didn't ask him. I was too excited, I guess."

"You can find out tomorrow," Christy suggested. "I'm glad your first day went so well."

"It was perfect, except for Slick Rick," Katie said, following Christy to the back of the store. "He came over to Santa's house and stood there for at least half an hour just smiling at me."

"Rick did?" Christy asked. "Why would he do that?"

"To drive me crazy. Why else?"

Jon, with the cash drawer in his hands, had joined them in the back room. Christy noticed a wry grin on his face.

"The old tease-her-best-friend trick," he muttered. "Worked a few times for me."

"What?" Katie asked.

"I don't think we want to know," Christy advised, pulling Katie out the back door. "Good night, Jon. See you tomorrow."

When they reached Christy's car, Katie said, "So, when are we going to make the cookies? We should make them Sunday afternoon; then we can take them with us to the Bible study that night."

"What are you talking about?"

"You know, the God-Lovers group at Rick and Doug's

apartment. We're going this Sunday night, aren't we?"

"Katie, where did you come up with all this?"

"Rick told me."

"When?"

"Well, I sort of talked to him on my break. He told me all about the weekend plans. Why? Didn't he tell you?"

Christy looked at Katie in disbelief. "Rick actually waited around for you, and you spent your break with him?"

"Yeah, so?"

"And he invited you to God-Lovers, and you really want to go?"

"Sure. Don't you? I think it'll be fun. I want to meet this Doug I've heard so much about." Katie plunged her felt hat and shoes into her bag and looked at Christy, who sat frozen in the driver's seat, the keys in her hand. "What's wrong?"

"Nothing," Christy snapped, swallowing all her confusion and surprise in one huge gulp. "Nothing at all."

Jamming the keys into the ignition, she started the car with a roar. Then she forced herself to ask calmly, "So, what kind of cookies should we make?"

CHAPTER TWO

Chocolate-Chip Rescue

"Well, what did your parents say?" Katie asked the next morning on the phone. "Can you go to God-Lovers?"

"I haven't asked them yet," Christy said with a sigh. "I have a feeling I already know what they'll say."

"Tell them I'm going," Katie urged. "My parents said it was okay. They even said I could have the car, and I don't have to be home until 11:00. Maybe if you tell your parents I'm driving, they'll let you go."

Christy felt a tinge of jealousy over Katie's freedom. She knew she shouldn't compare. Still, it didn't seem fair.

"I was thinking," Christy said, "maybe we should try to go next Sunday night because Christmas break starts then, and we won't have any school on Monday. This Sunday is still a school night for me, and I'm supposed to be home by 9:00."

"Why don't we go both weeks? Or at least try to go both weeks. I'm really looking forward to it, and I'd like it if you could come with me this week."

Christy realized Katie planned to go whether Christy went with her or not. That hurt. After all, Rick and Doug were her friends. Why should Katie feel so welcomed into their group without Christy there?

"I have to get ready for work," Christy stated abruptly. "I don't want to be late again like yesterday." She said it with a jab, as if she wanted Katie to take the hint that it was her fault Christy had been late.

"Oh, you're right! It's already after 10:00, and I'm not dressed yet. Hey, do you want to meet at the food court on our lunch break?"

"Okay," Christy said. "I usually have my break at 1:00."

"Great! I'll meet you at the donut bar at 1:00 unless I can't get away then. Bye!" Katie said cheerfully before hanging up.

Yeah, or unless Slick Rick comes to bug you again. Christy had thought through the situation with Rick a dozen times. None of it made sense. She could believe the part about Doug wanting Rick to invite Christy to God-Lovers, but why did Rick wait around to have dinner with Katie—especially since he had told Christy he couldn't meet her during her break?

She jumped into the shower and quickly washed her hair, debating whether to approach her parents this morning about driving to San Diego with Katie or to wait until that evening. She knew they would say no either way. Why bother asking at all?

It ended up taking a half hour to get ready for work, which meant she barely had enough time to fly out the door with a "See you later" tossed over her shoulder to Mom and Dad.

Her morning continued at a frenzied pace. She couldn't believe it was already 1:00 when Jon asked if she wanted to take her lunch break.

Christy arrived at the donut bar at 1:04. Katie wasn't in sight. After waiting 10 minutes, Christy realized if she didn't get in line and order lunch, her break would be over. She was starving and had no trouble deciding on the French bread pizza, even though that line was one of the longest.

While she waited in line and then sat down to eat her pizza, Christy kept scanning the noisy plaza for Katie. For some reason, she half expected to see Rick as well. She saw neither and had to hurry back to the pet store. If she had had more time, she would have visited Santa's house to watch Katie in action. Or maybe even spot Rick there.

Stop it! she reprimanded herself. *Why are you thinking like this about Rick and Katie? Get your head out of the garbage can, girl! It stinks in there.*

From the minute she stepped back into the shop until she left at 6:00, business remained steady. She felt glad the afternoon had zoomed by. Since Katie never appeared, Christy thought she had better check in on her before going home.

The line at Santa's house wrapped halfway around the large snow scene. In the middle of the display stood a three-sided cottage complete with fake snow, icicles, and mechanical elves who were wired to continually wrap presents and paint red stripes on candy canes.

Christy thought the snow looked funny at this Southern California mall where most of the shoppers wore shorts. The jolly, rotund Santa sat on his throne with a camera positioned in front of him.

And there, next to the camera, danced Katie. The eyes of the toddler on Santa's lap followed her antics with obvious glee. "Look at Rudolph!" Katie said in a squeaky voice, holding up a reindeer hand puppet. "He's about to fly!"

Katie swooped the puppet forward, beeping Rudolph's red nose on the little boy's nose. She ducked as the bright flash went off, capturing the child's big smile.

No wonder Rick stuck around. I could watch her for hours, too. She sure has a knack for this. Why was I getting so jealous and worried about Rick being interested in Katie? That's ridiculous!

As the next child approached the place of honor, Christy caught Katie's attention and called out, "I'm going home now. Call me, okay?"

Katie called back, "We've been so busy! I'll be here another hour. Do you want to bake cookies at my house tonight or tomorrow?"

Aware of the photographer's disapproving glare, Christy shrugged and said, "Call me when you get home, okay?"

Katie nodded and waved. She reached into a basket next to the camera, pulled out a squeaky snowman, and went back to her make-the-baby-smile routine.

Katie finally called Christy at 9:30, full of excitement. "I just got home, and you'll never believe what happened! You know the photographer? He offered me a job! After Christmas. He wants me to work at his studio when he does children's portraits. He says I'm the best assistant he's ever had! And get this: He offered to pay me double what I'm getting now!"

"That's great, Katie! Good for you." Christy tried to make her voice sound light and sweet, even though she didn't feel that way. No one had ever said she was the best at anything or offered to double her salary.

"And the best part of all is that I don't have to wear a costume," Katie said, laughing. "I did tell him the ears were real, though, but he promised me his company didn't discriminate against big ears. I'm so excited! I can't believe he hired me just like that."

"That's really great, Katie."

"Sorry it took me so long to get home. I know it's too late to make cookies tonight, but why don't we do it tomorrow? Can you come over here right after church?"

"Hang on," Christy said. "Let me ask my mom."

Christy covered the phone and called to her mom in the other room, "Mom, is it okay if I go to Katie's after church tomorrow to bake cookies?"

"Sure, that would be fine," Mom called back. "I have some butter and chocolate chips in the freezer you can take with you."

The next afternoon, as the girls began their cookie baking, Christy realized it was a good thing she had brought the extra chocolate chips. Katie, who admitted being unable to stay in the same room with any form of chocolate without devouring it, had already made a dent in her supply.

"Pretend they aren't there," Christy advised, "and measure the flour for me."

"You're asking me to ignore them?" Katie asked, looking longingly at the chips spilling from the open bag. "Look at them, Christy. Look at those sad little chips with their tiny, little brown elf caps. Can't you hear them?"

Katie bent closer to the counter, her hand cupped behind her ear. "They're saying. 'We're cold out here, wearing nothing but our tiny elf caps. Please let us come inside your warm tummy!' "

With her most sympathetic expression, Katie pleaded with Christy. "How can you be so cruel as to leave them there, alone in the cold, shivering?"

"Oh, all right!" Christy said, scooping up the bag and twisting the top to lock the remaining chips inside. "Just these orphans here on the counter. Their brothers and sisters are mine!

And I shall keep them as my prisoners while you measure the flour.''

"Oh, thank you, thank you! I knew you had a tender heart. Come, little chips," Katie said, brushing them into her hand, "time to go for a ride on a big slide! Ready? Go!" She dropped the handful into her mouth.

"Murf eill bumph dhl grayde," Katie said.

"What?" Christy asked.

With a swallow and a lick of her lips, Katie repeated, "I said, they feel better already."

Christy shook her head. "You know, Katie, you really should be in drama. You're going to be the next Lucy or Rosie, I just know it."

"It's my red hair. When the first words you recognize as a child are 'carrot top,' you quickly figure out you're not in line for future Miss America."

"Oh, yeah? Well, that's not what Glen seemed to think this morning. Isn't this the first time he's actually sat by you at church?"

"You noticed, huh?"

"Noticed! How could I not notice? He acted as if you were the only one in the whole Sunday school class. I'd say that shy guy has come a long way!"

"Going a long way is more like it," Katie said with a sigh. "He's leaving as soon as school is out this Friday. His parents are going on a two-week trip to Oregon to raise their support so they can go back to Ecuador in the spring."

"Then he won't be around for Christmas," Christy said, feeling sorry for Katie. Glen was a nice guy, and Christy thought he and Katie were good for each other.

Katie poured the flour into the mixing bowl. "I bought him a

CD yesterday at the Christian bookstore. I was going to give it to him this morning, but he didn't get me anything, and I felt strange giving him a present, so I didn't."

"Wait a minute," Christy said, pausing from her batter mixing. "If I remember correctly, you were the one last Christmas who convinced me to give a gift to Rick, even though I barely knew him. I think it's your turn to give a guy a present in the church parking lot."

"No, no, no. You see, you provided both of us with a very good learning experience last year. I learned from your embarrassment, and therefore, I do not need to repeat the same mistake you already made on behalf of both of us."

"Oh, right! That is such a wimp-out, Katie. First of all, Glen is not Rick, so it won't be the same kind of mistake. Second, Glen probably didn't give you a gift because he has no money, right? And third . . . " Christy hesitated. "I forget what third is. But I still think you should consider it missionary support and give Glen the CD. He'll have something to listen to on his long trip to Oregon."

Katie thought for a minute and said, "I guess you're right, as always. Christmas is supposed to be about giving, not receiving, right? I hate it when you like a guy, and you can't tell if he likes you back."

"Believe me," Christy agreed, "I know how that feels. You should do what you've told me to do—be honest about your feelings and see what happens."

"All right, I'll give Glen the CD. But when? He's leaving on Friday."

"He usually goes to church on Sunday nights, doesn't he? Why don't you give it to him tonight?"

"What about the trip to San Diego?"

"Katie," Christy confessed, "I can't go to San Diego tonight. I never even asked my parents. I knew they'd say no."

"I thought you worked it out with them!"

"No," Christy admitted, shaking her head, "but I still wanted to make the cookies. I thought we could mail them to the guys. Or if you go by yourself tonight, you can deliver them."

Katie pulled the cookie sheets out from the cupboard and slammed them on the counter. "What you're really saying is that you don't want me to go down there by myself because Doug and the others are all your friends. If you can't go, then you don't want me to go. Right?"

"It's not like that, Katie." Christy caught herself before she made up a lie. "Well, maybe that's part of it. I do feel left out. But I only know Doug and Rick. I don't know anyone else there. I just wanted us both to be able to go. That's all."

Katie had been staring at the floor while Christy was talking. She looked up and flashed her green eyes at Christy. "Okay, I'll wait and go when you can. And I'll give Glen the CD tonight."

"Are you sure?"

"Yes, I'm sure."

"Thanks, Katie. You're the most understanding friend in the world."

"Wait; there's a condition. If I can do all that, then you can at least ask your parents about going to San Diego next Sunday."

"I will," Christy promised. "They'll say no, but I'll ask anyway."

"Christy, you won't know until you ask!"

Two hours later, as Christy walked in the front door with a plateful of cookies in her hand, the phone rang.

"I'll get it," she called out, reaching for the receiver and placing the cookies on the kitchen counter. "Hello?"

"Hi, Christy? This is Doug."

"Doug, hi! Guess what I have for you?"

"I hope it's cookies!"

"Yep. Katie and I made them this afternoon for you guys. I'll
mail them to you tomorrow."

"I was hoping you were bringing them with you tonight. Rick
said he gave you the message."

"He did," Christy said, "but I can't come. I'm sorry, Doug. I
really wanted to, and hopefully I'll be able to another time." She
lowered her voice. "My parents aren't in favor of my driving all
that way at night and everything."

"I wish I'd known that," Doug said. "I could've given you a
ride."

"That's okay, Doug. It's kind of a long way for you to have to
come."

"I wouldn't have minded a bit. Actually, I should have called
you earlier. You see, tonight is our last God-Lovers. We won't
meet again until next semester starts up. Probably the end of January."

"Oh, I didn't know, Doug. I'm sorry. Now I really feel bad."

"I should have called you earlier," Doug said. "But, hey, we
have a huge Christmas break starting next week. We can all get
together and do something then. Are you going to be at your aunt
and uncle's in Newport Beach like you were last year?"

"I'm not sure yet what we're doing. I could probably make
arrangements at work and ask my aunt if I could stay with her."
Christy thought of how fun it would be to get together with her
Newport Beach friends again. Last Christmas she had had breakfast on the beach with Todd.

Todd was so different from any other guy she had ever known. The last two years of her life were filled with memories of him: her first kiss; a trip to Disneyland on her birthday; the vacation last summer on Maui; long talks; and many ups and downs. She thought of New Year's Eve last year when she and Todd went to a party in Newport Beach at their friend Heather's house. At midnight Todd had given her a gold ID bracelet with the word "Forever" engraved on it and had kissed her.

While she was dating Rick, he had "borrowed" the ID bracelet and traded it for a clunky silver one that said "Rick." Her relationship with Rick had its share of rough water, but when she found out he had taken Todd's bracelet and sold it, she broke up with him immediately.

Christy had faithfully made payments at the jewelry store to retrieve her gold bracelet. Then one day she went to make a payment and found out some guy, who wished to remain anonymous, had paid it off.

She still didn't know who it was. At first she suspected Jon, her boss. He denied it when she asked him. Katie thought it might have been Rick, trying to make up for being such a jerk. For a while Christy wondered if somehow Todd had found out and paid it off.

She glanced at her bracelet, now secure on her right wrist, and asked Doug, "Have you heard anything from Todd? Did he say when he's coming back from Hawaii?"

"No, I haven't," Doug answered slowly. "We need to be praying for him though, because the next two weeks are his big competition weeks at Waimea. He'll either make the pro surfing circuit or drop out."

"If he doesn't make it, does that mean he might come home?" Christy asked, trying not to sound too hopeful.

"Who knows. He might stay at U of H for the next semester. Or he could be on a plane back right now. You never know with Todd."

Well said, Doug. I couldn't have expressed it better myself. You never know with Todd. Looking at her bracelet again she thought, *He could be on a plane right now. You never know!*

CHAPTER THREE

Opposites Don't Attract, Do They?

Christy woke up Monday morning with a sore throat and thought about how wonderful it would be to stay in her cozy bed all day. But she knew that, with only five more school days until Christmas break, she couldn't afford to miss any of her tests or get behind in her homework.

So she made an agreement with herself. *If I don't feel better after I take a nice, hot shower, then I'll go back to bed.*

The shower seemed to perk her up, and she went to school with a package of Mom's cough drops in her purse. She actually felt okay until lunch when she told Katie about Doug's phone call.

"So we missed our one opportunity," Katie said flatly.

"They'll start up again in January," Christy replied defensively. "I didn't know that was their final meeting."

"I'm not blaming you," Katie said. "I'm bummed, that's all. I had such a great feeling about being invited to a college campus and being considered on 'their' level."

"Is that why you were so eager to go?"

"Sure! Didn't it make you feel a little grown-up and, you know . . . kind of like the big kids were saying, 'Red Rover, Red

Rover, send Katie and Christy right over'?"

"Not really, but I can see what you mean. Don't strangle me, but for a while I was thinking you wanted to go because of Rick."

Katie dropped her candy bar on her lunch bag and said, "Christy, how could you even think that?"

"I don't know. Maybe it's because I know Rick. He likes a challenge. You know that. I guess it seemed after our encounter with him in the mall parking lot that you became sort of a challenge to him."

"Challenge or no challenge, Rick isn't exactly my favorite person."

"I know."

"Rick and I couldn't be more opposite," Katie stated, snatching up her candy bar and chomping into it for added emphasis.

To herself, Christy muttered, "Sometimes opposites attract."

"I heard that," Katie said. "Now can we talk about something else? Like the way Glen hugged me last night when I gave him the CD?"

"Oh, Katie! I'm sorry; I meant to ask you what happened. Tell me, tell me!"

"There's not much to tell. I gave him the CD after church last night, and he hugged me and said thanks. His mom was standing right there. It wasn't a big deal."

Christy's eyes scanned Katie's for more details.

"That's it," Katie said. "It was nice. I'm glad I gave it to him, but I wouldn't write a love sonnet about the experience. Speaking of sonnets, have you read that 13-page sonnet for English yet?"

Christy shook her head and slowly sucked her boxed orange

juice through the thin straw. It surprised her that Katie wasn't more excited about Glen. She didn't seem to be as interested in him as she had been a month ago.

Christy watched and listened to Katie the rest of the week. She didn't mention Glen once. Christy thought it best to wait for the right time before bringing up his name.

It was a grueling week of homework and three huge exams. By Friday Christy was so eager for school to end that she spent her last class writing out Christmas cards and working on her Christmas shopping list.

Half the class had ditched, and the teacher sat on the edge of his desk showing a clump of students his famous card tricks. Christy hoped to finish all her Christmas cards so she could mail them from work that night. With only a week left before Christmas, she hoped they would arrive on time. Alissa's card was going to Boston, and Paula's would be sent to Wisconsin, but the rest of her friends were in California, so their cards should arrive before the big day.

But what should she do about Todd? She had a card addressed to him at his address on Oahu, but would he get it if he were surfing all week like Doug said?

And what about a present? Last year she had painted a surfer on a T-shirt for him. He probably liked it, because she had seen him wear it several times.

This year a painted T-shirt seemed like a dumb present. She was surprised she had thought it was such a great idea last year. Maybe she should just send him a card. It was probably too late to mail anything to Hawaii anyway. She should have thought of all this much sooner.

The final bell rang, and everyone cheered and joked, saying, "See you next year!"

Christy stuffed her cards in her bag and met Katie at Christy's locker as planned.

"Ready?" Christy asked. "I'd like to get to work a little early so I can mail my Christmas cards."

"I have everything," Katie said. "Let's go. Thanks for giving me a ride again. If my brother doesn't get his car fixed soon, I'm going to make my parents give him an ultimatum. He doesn't even ask. He just takes off in my car as if I don't have places to go, people to see."

"Why don't you ask your parents to get his car fixed for him as his Christmas present?"

"That's a good idea," Katie agreed as Christy unlocked the car doors.

"By the way," Katie asked, "what are you getting Rick this year?"

"Rick? Nothing!"

"Not even a card?"

"Well, maybe a card. I was going to send one to Doug, and I was thinking about adding Rick's name to it. I want to talk to him face-to-face and settle everything between us. I don't think a card would do much good."

"Sounds wise," Katie said, humming to herself the rest of the way to the mall.

Now Christy's curiosity was up. As they walked into the mall, she asked, "Katie, why did you ask if I was sending Rick a Christmas card?"

"Oh, no reason," she said.

Christy wasn't convinced. She felt suspicious the rest of the evening. It still bothered her that Rick had hung around and talked to Katie last Friday, and yet he hadn't given her a time when they could sit down and talk.

Maybe it was up to her to set the time. She had Rick's phone numbers in San Diego and at his parents' home. She could call him and make him talk to her. But by the time Christy arrived home from work, all her fiery determination had died down to the same barely warm embers she had felt ever since they broke up. She would wait for him to call.

To her surprise, the next morning he did.

"Hi," Christy said, not at all sure what to say next. She decided to let him do the talking.

"Nice being out of school for Christmas, isn't it?" Rick said.

"Yes. Yes it is."

"Well, are you working all next week?"

"I work Wednesday all day, but I have the rest of the week off."

"So, Monday would be good to get together and talk," Rick said. It sounded more like a statement than a question.

"I think so. What time?"

Rick was silent for a minute. Christy wondered if she had asked the wrong question. For this to work, it had to be Rick's idea that they get together. She refused to give him any cause to think of her as one of his many old girlfriends who was trying to get back together with him.

"I don't know," Rick said suddenly. "I'll call you."

"Okay," Christy replied.

Then he hung up.

At first his abruptness made her mad. Then she thought of how he had sounded as though he were trying to figure out how to talk to her normally. The whole time she had known him, he had been a smooth talker with lots of promises and flattery. Maybe Rick didn't know how to talk to her without an ulterior motive. Or maybe he was changing, and his new, shy side was coming out. Did he really want to get together and talk, or was he doing this just for her? Could it be that hard for him to switch from girlfriend to friend and let their relationship go on, even if he didn't always have control?

I guess I'll find out Monday, Christy thought and hurried to get ready for work.

She arrived at the pet shop around 10:45. It was clear that the Christmas rush had begun. Christy rang up purchases for nearly two hours without a let-up. Most of the sales were the seasonal promotional stuff like kitty stockings filled with catnip and reindeer horns on a headband for a dog.

Christy didn't mind that it was so busy. She actually entered into the spirit of things and told the customers, "Merry Christmas" when she handed them their bags.

Around 1:00, Beverly, the other pet shop employee, came to relieve her at the cash register.

"Jon said he wanted to see you in the back," Beverly told her.

Uh-oh. Sounds like I'm in trouble.

Jon was slicing open a box when she stepped into the back room.

"You wanted to see me?"

"Yeah. Have a seat. I wanted to talk to you about the way you've been saying 'Merry Christmas' to all the customers."

"Yes?"

"Well, Christy, not all of our customers celebrate Christmas. It could be offensive to them," Jon said.

"I'm only trying to be nice," Christy said defensively. "It didn't seem to bother anyone. Most of them said 'Merry Christmas' back. I think they like hearing it."

"Now don't be defensive," Jon said. "Change it to 'Seasons

Greetings,' and no one will be offended, okay?''

Christy started to nod, but then she realized that deep inside, it wasn't okay.

"Okay?" Jon said again, looking for her agreement.

"No, it's not really."

Jon looked surprised and waited for her to explain.

Christy bravely put her thoughts into words. "Remember once you told me that if people believe something they should take a stand and not be sneaky about it?"

"Well, yes," Jon said. "That sounds like something I'd say. I'm sure I wasn't referring to this, though."

"It applies to this," Christy said firmly, before she lost all her nerve. "At least to me, it does. It's not just a season that I'm celebrating. I'm celebrating Christ's birthday, and that's what Christmas is. Everybody knows that. How can that be offensive?"

"Christy, that might be what you believe, but that's not what everyone else believes."

"Then if they don't believe it, why can't they accept what I believe and say their own 'Seasons Greetings' back to me?"

"Okay, okay!" Jon said. "You win. You believe something, you're taking a stand for it, and I have to admit, I admire that. Go ahead. Stick with the 'Merry Christmas.' How much can it hurt?"

"Thanks, Jon."

"That's okay. Now why don't you take your lunch break? It's been nonstop all morning. If you don't get away now, you might not get a chance."

Christy was about to leave when she realized that because it had been so busy, Jon hadn't taken a lunch break, either.

"I'll get something and bring it back," Christy said. "And what do you want me to bring for you? It's my treat."

Jon looked up, surprised at her offer. "Are you serious?"

"Of course I'm serious. I got paid today, remember? So, what do you want?"

"Well, you know the Chinese food place in the food court?" Christy nodded.

"Go there and ask for Yun. Tell him Jon wants his usual. To go," Jon said, reaching for his wallet.

"Got it," Christy said. "Hey, put your money away. This is on me, remember? Think of it as my early Christmas present to you." She emphasized the "Christmas" and looked at Jon for his reaction.

For a few seconds he met her gaze, a slight smile lighting his face. Putting his wallet back, he said, "Thanks, Christy. And Merry Christmas to you, too."

Jon's response made her feel good all over as she quickly wound her way through the crowded mall to the food court. The line at the Chinese food counter was long.

During the five-minute wait to get to the front of the line, Christy forgot whom she was supposed to ask for. She scanned her brain, trying to find the name, and felt completely flustered when she reached the front.

"Hi," she said to the aproned clerk. "Do you know Jon?" The dark-haired guy looked at her funny and said, "Egg foo yong?"

"No, at the pet store. Do you know the guy who works at the pet store? His name is Jon." She could tell she wasn't getting any-where.

A slender man with a kind face stepped up behind the clerk and asked, "Is there a problem?"

Christy noticed the name on the man's tag.

"Yun!" she said excitedly. "You're Yun."

The man looked at the clerk and then at Christy. "Yes, I'm Yun. Have been as long as I can remember."

Christy laughed, relieved that she hadn't blown her errand of kindness. "I work at the pet store, and I'd like to order the usual for Jon."

"Oh, Jon!" Yun said, his face lighting up. "Sure. I'll get it for you. Will there be anything else?"

Christy hadn't thought of what to order for herself. "I guess I'll have an egg roll. Oh, wait. Do you have those little, um . . . what are they called?"

The clerk stared blankly at her, and she became aware of the stares from the people standing in line behind her.

"Forget the egg roll. I'll just have the sweet and sour shrimp. Oh, and some rice. A small. Rice, I mean. A small rice and a small sweet and sour shrimp. Please."

The clerk handed her the ticket, and motioning to the right, he said, "Pay down there."

Turning to another employee near him, the clerk rattled off something that made the other guy laugh.

No need for a translation on that, she thought. *I'd know "ditz" in any language.*

Christy paid for the food, trying to be calm and gracious as Yun handed her the large bag.

"Here you go," he said, "And please tell Jon 'Merry Christmas' for me."

Christy smiled and nodded; she would love to tell Jon that Yun wished him a Merry Christmas.

As she headed back toward the pet store, she tried to decide if she should hurry back or take a detour to see Katie, which had been her original plan for her lunch break. The smell of the hot food made the decision for her. She would wait and see Katie after work.

When Christy entered the pet store, she motioned to Jon by lifting the bag and tilting her head toward the back room.

"Go ahead," Jon said, pouring a box of rubber dog bones into a basket by the front register. "I'll be there in a minute."

She eagerly set up the Chinese picnic on the card table in the back room. Drawing in the feast's wonderful scent, she felt hungry enough to eat it all herself.

"I brought you a lunch guest," Jon said as he stepped into the back room. Christy peered around him, expecting to see Katie.

"Doug!"

"Hi, Christy!" he said, wrapping his arms around her in one of his famous hugs. "Guess I came at the right time."

Christy was so surprised she was at a loss for words.

"You two go ahead and dig in," Jon said. Patting Doug on the shoulder, he added, "Help yourself to whatever you like. It's Christy's treat."

Doug pulled up a folding chair and said, "I already ate. Sure smells good, though. Maybe I will have a little rice. I stopped in only for a second. I'm on my way home for the holidays, and I wanted to see if we could set up something for next week." With a peek inside one of the white boxes, Doug asked, "What is this?"

"I'm not sure. It's Jon's 'usual.' This one is sweet and sour shrimp, and this one is rice," Christy explained. "You want some?"

"Sure," Doug said, holding up a paper plate for Christy to scoop the rice and shrimp onto.

She divided up the food and was about to take a bite when

Doug asked, "Do you want to pray?"

"Oh, sure," she said, bowing her head and waiting for Doug to pray for her the way Todd always did. It was silent.

"Go ahead," Doug whispered. "You pray."

"Oh, you meant me," Christy said, bowing her head once more and quickly thanking God for the food.

When she looked up, Jon stood a few feet away.

"Don't mind me," he said, reaching for a box of doggie treats.

I wonder what Jon thinks of all this? Of Doug and me praying and everything?

"Remember how we all went ice-skating last year?" Doug asked. "Do you think we should do that again this year?" Christy vividly remembered that wild day with its mix-ups. She also remembered skating with Doug, supposedly to make Todd jealous. In the end, Doug turned out to be a great skater, and they had had a lot of fun together.

"Ice-skating would be fun. Or we could go to the movies, or maybe Heather would want to have another New Year's party," Christy suggested.

"Hey, you know what would be fun?" Doug said, swallowing a mouthful of rice. "We should all go to the Rose Parade!"

"That would be great!" Christy's face broke into a huge smile. "We always used to watch the Rose Parade in Wisconsin, and I grew up dreaming about going someday. Seeing all that sunshine when you're bundled up and it's snowing outside makes California seem like paradise."

"The parade is a lot of fun," Doug said. "A bunch of us went two years ago and slept overnight on the street so we could have front row seats. It's time for us to go again. That takes care of New Year's. What else do you want to do next week? Do you want to get together on Monday? I thought it'd be fun to go sledding up in the mountains."

What's Doug asking me? Is he thinking about a group thing, or is he asking me out? Rick wanted to get together Monday. What do I say?

"Monday?" she asked.

Doug nodded and bit into a chunk of sweet and sour celery.

"By any chance, did you and Rick talk about this? Because he said something about getting together on Monday. Did you guys already have something in mind to do as a group?"

"Oh, well, not really." Doug looked disappointed. "I didn't know you and Rick were, you know . . . getting together. I didn't know you already had plans."

"We don't really. Rick suggested we get together Monday, but maybe he meant we could all get together, like you're saying. We could all go sledding."

Christy wasn't sure she was doing the right thing here, forfeiting her opportunity to talk with Rick. But the thought had entered her mind that if Katie came along, she might hit it off with Doug, and the two of them could kind of be together, and she could be with Rick.

"I'll stop by his house when I leave here. We'll see what we can come up with. Rick said you had a friend named Katie?"

"Yes, I wanted to invite her along to whatever we end up doing. Is that okay?"

"Great," Doug said, his warm smile returning. "The more the merrier! I'll look forward to meeting her."

Doug really was a great guy. Good-looking, too. Tall like Todd but with broader shoulders and a more boyish face. Doug wore his sandy blond hair short on the sides, and he always looked as if he'd just combed it. He had a warm smile with perfectly straight teeth. The more Christy thought about it, the more she thought

Doug and Katie might make a good couple. Doug had been interested in Tracy, one of Christy's beach friends. But that was a year ago, and it didn't appear that anything had come of Doug and Tracy's brief time of dating.

"I'll call you tomorrow afternoon and let you know what we've got going, okay? When are you coming up to Newport Beach?" Doug asked.

"I don't know yet. I'll find out before you call tomorrow," Christy promised.

Just then Jon walked in, and Doug rose to leave.

He shook hands with Jon and said, "Nice meeting you." Then he squeezed Christy's shoulder and said, "I'll call you tomorrow. See you."

Jon sat down and surveyed the feast. "So, where're the fortune cookies?"

Christy fished her hand around inside the bag until she found the two cookies. "Here you go."

Jon picked up the wooden chopsticks and started in on a box of the "usual," scooping up the noodles like a pro.

"You read yours first," he said.

Christy cracked open one of the cookies and read, " 'You do not yet realize what is before you.' That's silly," she said. "What's before me? A bunch of Chinese food. I think I'm capable of realizing that."

Jon shook his head, his mouth full of noodles. Pointing his chopsticks at Christy he said, "It's not what's before you at this moment. It's what was sitting here before you, before he walked out the door."

"Doug?" Christy asked, giving Jon a skeptical look. "I don't realize what Doug is? Of course I do. He's just Doug. He's always been there. What am I supposed to realize?"

Jon raised his eyebrows and glanced at Christy out of the corner of his eye. He didn't say a word but kept looking at her as he jabbed his chopsticks into the box of noodles and stuffed them into his mouth, slowly sucking in one long, stray noodle.

CHAPTER FOUR

I'm Not Dreaming
of a White Christmas

On Sunday after church, Christy's family sat down to eat the roast chicken Mom had put in the oven on low that morning. Several weeks had passed since they had all sat down like this to a traditional Sunday family dinner. Everyone had been running in different directions, especially Christy.

"Your father and I have an announcement to make," Mom said as she passed Christy the spinach. "We talked with your Uncle Bob and Aunt Marti last night, and they've invited us to join them for a white Christmas!"

"What?" Christy asked, dropping her fork. "You mean we're going back to Wisconsin for Christmas? We can't! I have to work, and I have a lot of other things going on. Why can't we go to Bob and Marti's in Newport Beach like last year?"

"Christy, will you give your mother a chance to explain?" her father said.

He was a large man with rust-colored hair and matching eyebrows, big hands, a gruff voice, and a tender heart. "No, we're not going to Wisconsin, although your grandmother wanted very much for us to come. Maybe we'll see her next year. This year we're going to a cabin in the mountains that Bob and Marti have rented, and we're spending six days in the snow!"

"Six days," Christy moaned. "That's almost half the vacation!"

Christy's mom, a short, round woman with a plain face, gave Christy a disapproving look. "Yes, six days. We're going as a family to spend the holiday together. Your friends and your job will still be here when we come back. This is your father's first vacation all year."

Christy knew the look on Mom's face. Hushed up, Christy focused her attention on the food before her.

This is the worst possible Christmas I could ever have. I won't get to talk to Rick. I won't get to go to the Rose Parade with Doug and everyone. This is awful!

"Cool!" Christy's little brother, David, said. "Do we still have our old toboggan? Christy, remember how we used to sled down that hill out by Mr. Jansen's meadow? Don't you want to go sledding again?"

Christy shot a camouflaged sneer at her 10-year-old brother.

"Mom," David yelped, "Christy looked at me!"

"Christy," Dad said in his firm voice.

"I'm just not real interested in sledding, that's all."

"Christy," Mom said, "it may take you awhile to get used to the idea, but we are going, and it will be a wonderful Christmas."

"Okay," Christy said without looking up.

A year ago she might have fussed and tried to wiggle her way out of going. She knew now it was better to agree and go along with the family plan, even if it wasn't her first choice.

"Try to have a better attitude," Mom advised.

"I have a good attitude," David said. He looked more like their dad every day. "When do we leave?"

"Wednesday," Mom said. "And I'm glad you're excited about it, honey."

"I can't go Wednesday," Christy interrupted as Mom smiled at David. "I have to work on Wednesday. We all had to agree to work one full day during vacation, and my day is Wednesday."

"Trade with someone," Dad said. "Find out who's working on Monday, and see if you can trade with that person. That way you can help your mother pack on Tuesday."

"But Dad, I can't work on Monday!" Christy spouted. "I already have plans."

"What kind of plans?" Dad asked.

"With Katie and some other people. We're going sledding. I hadn't asked you yet, but I was going to."

Mom and Dad exchanged the type of look that only parents know how to give each other.

"You just said you didn't want to go sledding with me," David said. Dramatically slapping his forehead, he said, "Women! They're all loony!"

Dad smiled, and Christy looked to Mom for support. "Mom, did you hear what David said? Why do you let him get away with stuff like that? Where does he learn these things? I never got away with talking like that when I was his age."

"David," Dad said, shaking his head to show his disapproval. Christy thought her dad still looked as though he were laughing inside.

"Okay, listen," Mom the peacemaker said, "why don't you call work and find out if you can trade days. That's the first step. After that we can decide about this group sledding trip."

"Okay," Christy sighed, excusing herself from the table.

"You're not finished, are you?" Dad asked. "You've hardly eaten anything."

"I'm not really hungry. May I be excused?"

"Sure," said Mom. "Go see what you can do about changing your hours."

Christy called Jon and explained the situation. She could tell by the noise in the background a lot of people were in the pet store. She realized this might not be the best time to ask him.

"Tomorrow," Jon said, after checking his schedule. "You can work tomorrow instead. I need you here from 10:00 to 6:00. See you then." He hung up before she had a chance to ask about any other options.

Well, there went my Monday.

Trudging down the hall to her bedroom, Christy closed her door and flopped onto her unmade bed, where she could pout in private.

Why does stuff like this always happen to me? Katie never has to go through this. She can do whatever she wants, whenever she wants. My parents are too strict! Now I'm never going to get to talk to Rick. And everybody is going to have a great day tomorrow, and I have to work. It's not fair!

The phone rang, and a minute later Mom called out, "Christy, telephone."

Oh, great. It's probably Doug calling with the final plans for tomorrow, and I have to tell him to count me out.

"Hello?"

"Hi, it's me," Katie's voice responded. "Guess who just called me?"

"Glen?" Christy ventured.

"No, he's long gone on his way to Oregon. Rick."

"Rick? My Rick? I mean Doyle?"

"Your Rick?"

"I didn't mean that," Christy said. "You know what I meant."

Then turning the tables, Christy asked, "What's he doing calling you anyway?"

"He said he tried you, but the phone was busy," Katie answered defensively.

"I was only on it for three minutes," Christy snapped back.

"What's with you?" Katie asked. "What are you so upset about? Rick? You're ticked off that Rick called me?"

"No, it's not that. I'd never expect him to call you, but Rick can call whomever he wants. That's not what I'm upset about."

"Then what is it? Did I do something?" Katie asked.

"No, it's my family. They've made plans to go to the mountains for Christmas, and we'll be gone for six days starting Wednesday. I don't want to go, but I don't have a choice." She spoke softly so no one would hear her.

"It won't be that bad, Christy. You'll probably have fun. You'll be back for New Year's, won't you? Rick said we're all going to the Rose Parade and sleeping overnight on the street. I'm so excited! I've always wanted to do that."

"I'll be back by then, but I don't know if I can talk my parents into letting me go, especially since the plans include sleeping on the street."

"You haven't asked them, though, have you?"

"Not yet," Christy admitted.

"You have to start asking about these things, Christy. One of these days they'll surprise you and say yes to something. But you'll never know because you never ask them! Now listen to me. I have a plan. Start by asking them about sledding tomorrow. That's what Rick called about. They decided to go to Big Bear, and we're meeting at his house at 8:00. It'll be an all-day thing."

"I can't go," Christy said flatly.

"How do you know? You haven't even asked."

"Yes, I did. They didn't give me an answer because I have to work tomorrow from 10:00 to 6:00. I had to trade my Wednesday hours because we're leaving for the mountains Wednesday. The only option Jon gave me was to work tomorrow."

"Oh."

"See? It's hopeless. You get to do whatever you want, whenever you want, and I never get to do anything."

"Christina Juliet Miller, I can't believe you said that!" Katie snapped. "Who was it that went to Palm Springs and Newport Beach and Hawaii? Was it Katie Weldon? I don't think so! Would you like to take another guess?"

Christy remained silent.

"The only exciting thing I've done in my whole life is go to Lake Tahoe with the ski club last Thanksgiving. Now all of a sudden I have a chance to go to places like San Diego and Big Bear, and you're mad about it."

"I'm not mad," Christy said.

"Then you're jealous. Why? Because some of your friends are being nice to me and including me in their group! Is that so hard for you to accept?"

"No, that's not it at all! I'm glad you're getting to know some of my beach friends. They're all terrific, and I know they'll like you. It's just that you're being included and I'm being left out."

"Not on purpose, Christy. We're both being included. You can't go, that's all."

"That's what I'm upset about. I want more freedom. I want my parents to trust me more. I don't want to be tied down to a job. And most of all, I don't want to have all these responsibilities."

Katie paused before summarizing. "You want to be treated like an adult while you still have the freedom to be a kid."

"Yes, something like that. Seems to work for you."

"Sometimes. Maybe that's what happens when you're the youngest of three kids. It's probably harder for you since you're the oldest, and you have to be the first to break into new territory. It'll be easier for David."

"Don't talk to me about David. He just got away with this stupid wisecrack at the table, and I know if I would've tried something like that at his age I would've been sent to my room."

"Like I said, it's easier on the younger kids in a family."

"It's still not fair."

"So, what's fair in life?" Katie challenged.

"I don't know," Christy mumbled. "Not much, I guess."

"God is fair," Katie added thoughtfully. "Things that happen to us aren't fair from our perspective. I think in the end God evens things out when we leave the results to Him."

"I guess so," Christy said with a sigh.

"Come on, Christy," Katie said, "snap out of it! You need an attitude adjustment, girlfriend. And quick!"

"Oh, thanks a lot! Now you sound like my mother."

"Then erase that from your memory," Katie said. "You don't need an attitude adjustment. You need a friend. And I just happen to be one."

Christy let a smile lift her lips out of their pout.

Since Katie couldn't see Christy's response over the phone, she ventured another offering to her friend. "Remember? We're peculiar treasures, you and me. We have to stick together. And I've decided that because you have to work tomorrow, I won't go to Big Bear either."

"No, Katie, you should go. I want you to go. Really! You stayed home from San Diego because of me and that turned out to be a mistake. Don't turn down this opportunity. Go! Have a good time."

"Are you sure?"

"Yes. But will you do me one favor?"

"Anything! What is it?"

"Make a huge snowball and smash it into Rick's face for me!"

"Oh, my!" Katie joked. "Getting a bit feisty here, aren't we? I thought Rick no longer had the power to fire up your feelings."

"You're right," Christy agreed. "Forget I said that. You go and have a wonderful time and forget I ever said anything about Rick. Pretend I never met him."

"Pretend you never met whom?" Katie teased. "Rick? Rick who? I don't recall Christy ever mentioning a guy by that name."

Christy laughed. "Thanks, Katie."

"No, thank you for inviting me into your group."

Christy was about to say it was originally Rick's idea to invite Katie to God-Lovers, but then she would be mentioning *that* name again, and she had more self-control than that.

"And we'll go to the Rose Parade together," Katie said. "You'll see. I'll call you when we get back tomorrow night, or if you're still at work I'll try to stop by."

"What about your job?" Christy asked. "I thought you had to work this week, too."

"I do. But since I worked every afternoon and evening last week, they gave me Sunday and Monday off."

"Of course," Christy muttered to herself after she hung up, "Katie has Monday off, no problem! Not me. She's getting all the breaks lately. Why is God paying special attention to her and ignoring me? Not that she doesn't deserve it, but I deserve it, too, don't I?"

Work on Monday wasn't too bad. Christy spent most of the

morning in the back room marking sale prices on Christmas specialty items. The work was easy, and she didn't have to deal with the mob of customers out front. Still, she felt sorry for herself, knowing that her friends were out having fun while she worked.

She had brought a sack lunch with her and didn't even leave the back room when Jon told her to take her break. Settling in at the card table with her peanut butter and honey sandwich, Christy picked up a magazine from Jon's mail pile.

Without realizing it, she had selected a surfing magazine. The cover copy announced, *This Month, the Big One's at Waimea.*

A picture of a gigantic wave dotted with at least a dozen miniaturized surfboards took up the rest of the cover. It looked as though a huge blue fist was about to curl up its fingers and crush the antlike surfers.

Christy quickly found the feature article and pored over the photos and details of the surfing competition to be held that month on Oahu's North Shore.

Todd. He's there right now. Doug said it was this week. Todd's surfing waves like this!

She turned back to the cover and tried to imagine Todd on his orange surfboard, in the clutches of the ominous wave monster. It frightened her. Todd could die, trying to surf a wave like that. He could die, and it would be weeks before any of them would ever know.

Oh, God, keep him safe! Protect Todd and don't let him get hurt. I want You to bring him home soon. Katie said You are fair. Please be fair to Todd and protect him. Don't do it for me, though. Do what's best for Todd. But keep him safe, please!

CHAPTER FIVE

Camera-Shy Christy

Christy looked at the wall clock behind the counter in the pet store. *Six o'clock. Time for me to get out of here. Where's Jon? I can't leave the register until he relieves me. I wonder if I should buzz him or just wait. He knows I'm off at 6:00.*

Two customers stood in line. She decided to hurriedly ring up their purchases, hoping no one else would join them in line. The first customer had a large aquarium tank that Christy found awkward to get into a bag.

"Have you got it?" she asked the customer as she placed it in his arms.

"Yes, I do now. Thanks."

"You're welcome. Merry Christmas!"

"Merry Christmas to you," the customer responded.

The next customer slapped a bag of birdseed on the counter and muttered, "Took you long enough."

Christy recognized him as a frequent customer who seemed to love to complain. She and Jon referred to him as "Mr. Grouch."

Quickly punching the buttons on the cash register, Christy

turned to the man with her brightest smile and said, "That will be $5.78, please."

The man handed her a five-dollar bill and a dollar and fumbled in his pocket. "Hold on, hold on. I have three pennies here somewhere."

His search produced two pennies and a button. "Hold on," he said, sounding even more irritated.

Christy remembered feeling some change in her jeans pocket earlier. She stuck her fingers in and found a penny, which she presented to "Mr. Grouch" with a smile.

"Here, I have an extra penny."

He scowled at her but ceased his pocket search. Christy quickly made the change and popped his birdseed in a bag. She handed it to him with another big smile and said, "Merry Christmas, Mr. Grou—"

Oh no! she thought in a panic, when she realized what she had done. *I almost called him "Mr. Grouch" to his face!*

The man snorted and strode into the mall as if he hadn't heard her or as if he didn't care.

Christy felt her cheeks burn red as she turned to the next customer, ready to ring up the person's purchase. To her surprise, that person was Doug.

"Hi. I didn't even see you come in. How was the sledding at Big Bear?"

Doug's cheeks were rosy from the wind. He wore a red plaid flannel shirt and bib overalls that made him look like a kid who had been outside playing all day.

"Awesome! We had a blast. Everyone is over at the pizza place across the street. Katie said you finished work at 6:00, so I thought I'd chance it and see if you could have pizza with us."

"She'd love to," Jon said, stepping behind the counter and reaching for the phone.

"Yes," he said into the phone, "we have four Japanese fighting fish, and they're on sale until Christmas."

Christy smiled at Doug and said, "I guess my boss says I have to go. Let me grab my stuff. I'll be right back."

She slipped behind Jon and scooted to the back room to retrieve her purse. What she really needed to do was call her parents, and the phone in the back would allow her more privacy. As soon as she was sure Jon was off the phone, Christy dialed her home number. Her mom answered.

"Hi, I'm getting off work right now, and I wondered if I could have pizza with Katie and some other people." *There. That wasn't so hard. Why do I make asking to go places so hard? Wonder what she'll say. At least Mom answered rather than Dad.*

Her mom asked where Christy wanted to go and who would be there. Then she said, "Sounds like fun, honey. Think you'll be home by 9:00?"

"Yes. So, it's okay?"

"Sure! Have a good time. Lock the car, and don't give anyone a ride home."

Christy hung up and thought how nice Doug was to include her in their get-together. Maybe she'd have a chance to talk to Rick. If not at the pizza place, then he might suggest they get together tomorrow before she left for the mountains. She didn't want to go through Christmas without resolving their relationship. Grabbing her backpack and jacket, Christy joined Doug up front, where he and Jon were laughing together.

"I'm parked out that way," Christy said, pointing behind her. "Do you want me to meet you at the pizza place?"

"Why don't we both go in my truck?" Doug suggested. "I

have a parking place right by the entrance. Then I'll bring you back here afterward to pick up your car."

"Okay," Christy said, fully aware of Jon's look of approval.

"Merry Christmas, Jon," Christy said as a customer stepped up to the counter. "I'll see you next year."

"That's right. You don't work again until the Saturday after New Year's. Hang on a second."

Jon totaled the customer's purchase of three doggie stockings and handed her the change. As soon as the woman stepped away from the counter, Jon pulled an envelope from the cash register drawer and handed it to Christy.

"May it never be said that I'm a total Scrooge. Here's your year-end bonus, Christy."

"Thank, Jon!" She felt horrible for not buying him anything for Christmas. Even a plate of cookies would have been nice.

"Oh, and just to make you really happy . . . " Jon cleared his throat and glanced around to make certain no one could hear him except Doug and Christy. "May you have a joyful celebration of the birth of your God."

Christy, full of surprise, glanced at Doug and then back at Jon. "Thank you, Jon. And may *you* have a joyful celebration of the birth of my God." Then leaning closer and touching Jon's arm, she quietly added, "And may He become your God, too."

Jon smiled his touché to Christy.

She waved and headed out into the crowded mall with Doug beside her and Jon's gaze following them.

"Amazing how irresistible you are," Doug said.

"What?"

"To Jon," Doug said. "There's something mysterious and appealing about a person who knows God and doesn't hide it. I can tell that you and Jon have talked about God, and Jon knows you're a God-lover. That's irresistible to people who don't know God."

"Oh," Christy said as they walked out the door to his truck. "I never thought of it that way. Jon knows how I feel about my relationship with God. He also knows I've been praying for him, and I think it makes him nervous."

"That's awesome," Doug said, unlocking the passenger door of his yellow four-wheel-drive truck.

Christy smiled to herself and climbed up into the seat while Doug jogged around the front of the truck and slid in on the other side.

"What?" he asked when he saw her grin.

"I can't believe you still say 'awesome.' That's one of the first things I remember about you when we met on the beach. Everything was awesome to you."

Doug laughed. He had a great laugh that came from a gurgling brook inside him, and when it splashed out, it refreshed those who heard it.

"Most things are awesome, when you think about them. It's because of God. He's an awesome God. I don't know a word that says it better."

Christy smiled back. It felt good to be with an old friend. It was a familiar, safe, contented feeling.

"Who ended up going with you guys today?" Christy asked.

"Your friend Katie, Rick, Heather, Tracy, and a guy named Mike, who's a friend of Rick's. We had an awesome time. Katie sure is fun. How come you never brought her up to Newport Beach?"

"I guess it never worked out. I'm glad she got to go with you guys. Sounds as though she fit right in."

"She did. What a sense of humor!"

Doug's words proved true as they stepped into the restaurant and spotted the group at a large booth in the back. Katie had something on her ears, and the rest of the group was cracking up at her antics.

As Doug and Christy approached the booth, Christy saw that Katie had poked the bottoms out of two Styrofoam cups and placed a cup over each ear. Using her best Santa's little elf voice, she was coaxing them all to smile for the camera.

"Hi!" Doug greeted the merry group.

Rick and Mike barely noticed them. Tracy and Heather, two of Christy's beach friends, acted happy to see Christy, but they were so busy laughing at Katie that they merely scooted closer together in the booth and patted the corner for Christy to sit down and enjoy the show. Doug pulled up a chair at the end of the booth.

Katie continued, unembarrassed and apparently unaware of how ridiculous she looked and sounded. Christy could never act like that.

"Ah," Katie squeaked as she pointed to Christy, "my wardrobe assistant. May I borrow your earrings?"

With all eyes on her, Christy unclipped her dangling earrings. They were little green gift boxes tied with red ribbons. Tiny bells on them jingled when she shook her head.

Christy reluctantly handed them to Katie. They weren't valuable earrings, but she had bought them with her own money. She worried that Katie might unwrap the little boxes now just to get a laugh, and that would be the end of her earrings.

"Perfect!" Katie chirped, snapping the earrings onto the large, outer rims of the Styrofoam cups. The earrings now hung from her handmade elf ears, and the bells jingled when she wobbled

her head back and forth. She looked so silly that even Christy
started to laugh.

Out of nowhere, a guy from their high school stepped in front
of their booth and snapped a picture of Katie. Katie, Christy, and
Rick recognized him as Fred, the school yearbook candid camera-
man.

"Fred!" the three of them exclaimed in unison.

"Great!" Fred said. "I bet the school paper will be interested
in using this as their January cover. I can see it now: *What I Did
During Christmas Vacation, by Katie Weldon, the Elf.*"

"Give me that camera," Katie squawked from her closed-in
spot in the booth. "I want that film destroyed. Get it, Rick!"

Rick stood up and spoke to Fred in a low voice. Fred smiled
and nodded his head. Before Christy knew what was happening,
Rick slid in next to Christy and, practically sitting on her lap,
wrapped his arm around her and pressed his cheek against hers
just as Fred snapped another picture and took off.

"Rick!" Christy shouted, pushing him off the edge of the
booth seat. "He's going to put that in the yearbook!"

Rick dusted himself off and strutted back to his spot at the
opposite end of the booth. "That's what I'm counting on, Killer."

Christy was furious. She wanted to tell Rick off right then and
there. He had no right to push himself on her as if he owned her.
Everyone was looking at her, waiting for her response. Even Mike,
whom she hadn't met yet, looked amused at her expense.

"Come on," Doug suddenly said, grasping Christy by the
wrist and urging her to her feet. "We haven't ordered our pizza
yet. Do you like Canadian bacon and pineapple?"

Christy rose and let Doug hold her wrist as he led her to the
order counter. Tiny tears bubbled up in her eyes as the anger over
what Rick did surfaced.

As soon as they rounded the corner and were away from the group, Doug put both hands on her shoulders and said softly, "Are you okay?"

Christy blinked the tears back, looked up at Doug, and nodded. "I guess so."

"Rick thinks the world of you; you know that, don't you? I mean, talk about a godly woman being irresistible! You are absolutely irresistible to him. He doesn't know how to act around you because you're so different from all the other girls he knows. He doesn't mean to hurt you, really."

"I wish I could believe you."

Doug brushed his finger across her cheek to stop a runaway tear. "The problem is that you two need to talk things out. I know having your relationship unresolved must be killing you. Having lived with Rick all semester, I know it was eating him alive. You both need to talk."

"I'd like to," Christy said, "but it hasn't worked out yet. I've told him I want to talk, but he can't seem to schedule it. We were supposed to talk today."

"Maybe you still can," Doug said, opening up his arms and welcoming Christy into his comforting hug. "You relax and leave everything up to ol' Uncle Doug."

CHAPTER SIX

Thanks a Lot, Uncle Doug!

By the time Christy and Doug returned to the booth, the first two pizzas had arrived, and everyone was eating as if nothing unusual had happened.

Katie had removed her elf ears, and the earrings, unscathed, waited on a napkin at Christy's place.

"I wish you could have come with us today," Heather said to Christy. "We had so much fun. These guys are maniacs!"

"Oh, right," Rick said, reaching for another piece of pizza. "And you three girls weren't a bunch of little maniacs yourselves on your run through the trees?"

Wispy, blonde Heather giggled and described to Christy the run the three girls had taken. They had bounced off the slick path and headed into a clump of trees. Somehow they managed to maneuver through the obstacle course and ended up at the bottom of the hill without a tumble or a scratch.

The group chattered between bites of pizza, comparing wild stories and reliving the day's events. It was clear they all had had a wonderful time.

Christy felt left out. The pizza she and Doug ordered finally arrived. She listened to everyone else laugh while she mechanically bit into the hot, gooey cheese, which burned the roof of her mouth.

Reaching for a glass of water, she guzzled it down. It only helped a little. The roof of her mouth still felt red hot. No one had noticed her emergency, which made her feel even worse. If she weren't there, the party would have gone on without her.

Then the teasing began. Rick called Katie "Speed," and everyone laughed. Christy had no idea why that was funny. When he called Katie "Speed" a second time, she seemed to blush.

Christy could tell Katie loved the attention. The name had something to do with a run Rick and Katie had taken together on an inner tube.

Now Christy was really hurting. Rick had called her "Killer Eyes" for more than a year. That was his nickname for her, and nobody else called her that. It had seemed so sacred and special to have a name placed on her by Rick Doyle. Not anymore. Now Katie had a Rick nickname.

The conversation switched to plans for the Rose Parade. Rick announced he was bringing a hibachi to barbecue their dinner, an ice chest, and his down sleeping bag.

"The girls should be responsible for the extra blankets and all the junk food," Rick said.

"Cookies!" Doug agreed. "You girls can bring lots and lots of cookies."

"How about it, Speed?" Rick asked Katie with one of his big smiles. "Think you can make us some more of those killer cookies?"

Oh, great! Christy thought. *My nickname has now been reassigned to a batch of cookies, and Speed over there is getting the credit for the last batch we made, which would have been chocolate-chip-less if I hadn't been there!*

The more the group talked, the more exciting the plans sounded. Christy really wanted to go. She would have to find a way to talk her parents into it.

Doug leaned over and asked Christy if she thought she would need a ride.

"I don't know. First I have to convince my parents to let me go." She smiled at Doug, appreciating his interest.

"Do you want me to talk to them?" Doug offered. "I can tell them about how things were the last time we went."

"Thanks, Doug. I'd better try first. I'll let you know what they say. We're going to be up in the mountains at a cabin for the next week. I'll call you when we get back."

"A cabin? That sounds pretty awesome."

"I guess."

Seeing Doug's sincerity made her realize how grumpy she must seem to him.

You're being a baby, Christy. Snap out of it. Join the fun instead of feeling sorry for yourself.

Christy was beginning to pull herself out of her dismal mood when Heather said, "I hate to be the one to break this up; it's been such a fun day. But Tracy and I have a long ride home, and we need to get going."

Everyone slowly slid out, and Doug said, "Mike, why don't you come in my truck with me? And Rick, would you mind dropping Christy off at the mall? Her car is still there."

Christy didn't look at Rick. She heard him say "Okay" in a casual way.

Rick positioned himself by the door, holding it open in such a way that all the girls had to pass under his arm. The first three girls played along, sliding past Rick with smiles and giggles.

But Christy froze. She couldn't play along. A clear memory made her motionless.

She had been to this same pizza place before with Rick and Katie, about a year ago on a Sunday after church. Katie had been the center of attention that time, too. And Christy remembered being quiet and thoroughly absorbed with Rick. That time she had passed under Rick's arm at the door and looked up into his brown eyes. She had thought she might melt. He had overwhelmed her with his charm.

She felt afraid to pass under his imaginary bridge tonight, lest he drop an invisible net over her heart and she become captured by him again. Her silent refusal must have come across loud and clear to him because he looked at her hard and then let the door go. It closed in Christy's face.

Jerking the door open for herself, Christy bustled through and joined the others in the parking lot. She would not let Rick get to her like this.

Why can't Rick agree to a middle ground for us? Why does it have to be all or nothing?

"So you'll take Christy back to the mall to get her car?" Doug repeated his question to Rick.

"Sure," Rick agreed, glancing over his shoulder at Christy and tossing her the car keys. "Get in."

He spoke the command in a lighthearted way, but the message was clear. Rick needed to be in control.

Does he have any idea how insulting he sounds? Is he doing this to me on purpose? Or is Doug right, and Rick really cares about me but can't show it because we broke up?

Christy obediently opened the door and slid into the comfortable, familiar passenger seat of Rick's red Mustang. She put his keys in the ignition and watched out the front windshield as

Rick hugged Heather and Tracy good-bye. Then he hugged Katie.

The three girls hopped over to Christy's window and motioned for her to roll it down. She had been so absorbed with her confrontation with Rick that she hadn't even said good-bye to them.

Tracy reached her arms inside the open window and squeezed in to give Christy a hug around the neck. "Call me, okay?"

Heather waved and said, "I can't wait to see you on New Year's Day! We'll get all caught up then."

Christy waved as Heather and Tracy left. Katie opened the door and said, "Scoot forward. I'll get in the back."

Like a wildcat protecting her territory, Christy didn't move an inch. She stared at her clueless friend and in a low growl said, "Why can't you go with Doug and Mike?"

Katie looked amazed. Then, appearing to have caught on, she said, "You know, I love sitting in the front seat of that four-wheel-drive truck, sandwiched between two good-looking men, my legs all squished in such a dainty fashion. I much prefer it to riding in the backseat of this old clunker."

Katie called out to the guys who were saying good-bye to each other, "Hey, Doug, wait for me. I'm the peanut butter!" Rick turned and walked toward his Mustang with long strides, his expression stern. Christy felt her heart pounding. Maybe this wasn't such a good idea, after all.

He lowered his large frame into the front seat and slammed his door. Without a word he reached for the keys. He seemed to know that Christy had put them in the ignition, as she had done on several occasions when they were dating.

The car roared to life, and Christy held on while Rick peeled out of his parking spot. He turned to look at Doug out of his side window and honked and waved while the car accelerated past Doug's truck.

Christy noticed a small car pulling into the parking lot. She yelled, "Look out!"

The other car swerved to the left. Rick jerked the steering wheel to the right. The tires squealed. With another jerk, he turned the car and kept accelerating out of the parking lot. He changed lanes twice before coming to an abrupt stop at the red light by the mall.

Christy didn't dare say a word. She could hear Rick breathing heavily, and she knew he was mad. He drove to the section of the parking lot where Christy usually parked and found her car without saying anything. Conveniently, there was an empty space next to Christy's car. Rick turned in with a squeal of the tires, slammed on the brakes, and cut the engine, all in one motion.

Suddenly, it was quiet. Very quiet. Miserably quiet.

Christy wanted to scramble out the door and escape to the safety of her own car. Then she'd show him that she could squeal her own tires as she peeled out of the parking lot and away from him.

She couldn't do that, though, because she knew this was what she had wanted for months: a chance to talk to Rick. She didn't think it would happen like this or that both their emotions would be at full throttle when they finally connected. Maybe it was a bad idea. The timing was off. She should wait for a better time.

"You wanted to talk," Rick said. "What did you want to talk about?"

Christy felt awful. "About us," she said softly. "But not like this. I don't want to talk when we're both so upset."

"I'm not upset," Rick said gruffly. "You wanted to talk, so talk."

"I . . . I'm not sure I can . . ." Her throat swelled shut, and she couldn't say a word. It took a gigantic effort to keep back the sudden deluge of hot, prickly tears.

They sat in silence for several minutes. Christy didn't dare move, lest the tears find a crack to slip through and spill down her cheeks.

Rick let out a deep sigh and, in a calmer voice, said, "I saw the car coming, Christy. I wasn't going to hit it."

"I know. I'm sorry."

"You don't trust me," Rick said. "You've never trusted me."

"That's not true."

"Yes it is. You don't trust me, and you've been afraid of me since the day we met. You never gave our relationship a chance." Christy tried to think of how to answer that. In some ways it was true. Rick overpowered her just because he was Rick. How could she explain that to him?

"Go ahead," Rick urged. "Admit that you never really made room in your heart for me."

Christy shook her head, trying to find the right words. Rick came on so strong. He made her feel things she had never felt with Todd. Todd would never push her like this. Why couldn't she talk to Rick the way she talked to Todd? Todd would understand her feelings.

"You never even gave me a chance, did you? Come on!" Rick said, raising his voice. "You don't trust me. Say it!"

"That's not true. I do trust you, Todd."

Everything froze.

Todd! Oh no! I called him Todd! What have I done? Rick will never understand.

Rick stuck out his jaw and slowly turned his head away from Christy as if he had been slapped in the face. Calmly, he opened his car door and with even steps walked to Christy's side and opened her door.

She followed his unspoken instructions, still in shock that she had done such a thing.

He stood firm, a few inches from her, and calmly stated. "I'm not Todd. I'm Rick."

"I . . . I know, Rick. I'm sorry. I almost called a customer Mr. Grouch at work today," Christy began, but nothing she could say right now would make things better. "I don't know why I'm so mixed up with names today."

Rick acted as if he hadn't heard her. With composure he said, "There will never be room for me or any other guy in your life until you've put him away."

He shut Christy's door, walked to his side of the car with deliberate steps, got in, and started up the engine. Before she could think of a way to stop him, he lurched the car from its parking spot, and with screeching wheels, he sped away.

Christy's mind raced with thoughts of what to do. Part of her wanted to speed off after him and make him pull over his car and listen to her. She would find a way to make him understand and forgive her blunder. Another part of her wanted to give up on Rick forever and be done with running from him or chasing after him.

With trembling hands, she unlocked her car door and drove home cautiously, afraid of her own emotions. The most frightening thing was that she couldn't cry. She hurt too much to shed a single tear.

Maybe Rick was right. Maybe she had held on to the dream of Todd for too long. How could she move forward when her life was filled with memories of him? Before she reached home, Christy knew what she had to do.

She walked in the front door, said hello to her parents, and then rummaged in the garage until she found just the right size box. With another smile and a "good night" to her parents, she locked herself in her bedroom and began by tearing the poster from the back of her door.

It was a poster from Hawaii—a certain memorable bridge over a waterfall. She tossed the gift from Todd in the box and went straight for her dresser, scooping up the Folgers coffee can, which held a dozen very dead carnations—the first flowers she had ever been given by a guy. The coconut Todd had mailed her from Hawaii was the next victim tossed into the open box. Then the cable-car music box from San Francisco, which always made her think of Todd. Next, another gift from Todd—a tiny, glass-blown Tinkerbell figurine from Disneyland—and then a T-shirt from her drawer that said "I Survived the Hana Road."

Christy snatched her Winnie the Pooh bear off her bed and was about to plunge him into the box when she stopped. Holding the pudgy stuffed animal at arm's length, she told him, "I'm sorry, but you have to go, too."

She looked at the Todd mementos in the box and then explained to Pooh, "I can't have all of you whispering to me in my sleep, telling me fairy tales about Todd. I'm a big girl now. I can't believe in fairy tales anymore." Christy tightly hugged Pooh. "Don't you see? What happened tonight with Rick was my fault. I should have sent you all away long ago."

With one last kiss, Christy stuffed Pooh into the box and closed the lid. As a hot tear escaped, she slid the box under her bed and out of her heart.

CHAPTER SEVEN

Snow Wars

Christy awoke the next morning feeling sad and alone. She ate some breakfast and then returned to her room to pack for the family's trip to the mountains. When the mail came, Mom brought three cards in for Christy. Christy examined the return addresses and opened the one postmarked "Escondido."

It was a Christmas card from Teri Moreno, a girl from school whom Christy had met last year during the cheerleading tryouts. Teri wrote at the bottom of the card, *May your celebration of our Savior's birth be filled with joy.*

Christy set it aside, feeling guilty for being in such an emotional slump. She opened the next card, which was from Alissa, an older girl she had met on the beach two summers ago. A long note on a separate sheet of paper fell out. Christy sat down to read it.

Dear Christy,

I'm having so much fun preparing for Christmas here in Boston! Since this is the first Christmas since I became a Christian, everything means so much more than it ever did. My mom is doing pretty well. She's gone without a drink for about three months. And she and my grandmother have been coming to church with me! I sent a present to baby Shawna yesterday. I think about her all the time and miss her so much. I know she belongs with her adoptive parents, and I know they love her as much as I do. Whenever I start to feel really bad about her, God gives me this unexplainable peace, and I feel as though I can keep going. I pray for you all the time, Christy. I hope your Christmas is full of love, and joy, and peace.

Always,
Alissa

Christy stared at the letter, amazed. Alissa's father was dead, her mother was a recovering alcoholic, Alissa had given up her baby girl for adoption, and the baby's father had died in a surfing accident. If anyone had a reason to be depressed, it was Alissa.

Compared with her, Christy had it easy. Yet Christy was the depressed one, and Alissa sounded full of joy and hope—at least on paper.

Christy had to admit that last summer when she sat beside Alissa on the beach and listened to her pray and ask God to forgive her and come into her heart, Christy had wondered if it was real. Now Alissa was trusting God for more things than Christy was.

Maybe that's my problem. I haven't prayed much about all the stuff going on in my life.

Not feeling quite ready to pray, Christy opened the third card, which was from Paula, her childhood friend in Wisconsin. Out tumbled a stack of photographs. They were pictures Paula had taken last summer when she and Christy were in Hawaii with Christy's mom, David, her aunt and uncle, and Todd. The first picture was a waterfall with a bridge across the top, the same waterfall in the poster Christy had taken off her door. The next picture was of Todd on the beach with his arm around a surfboard. David stood on the other side of the surfboard trying to imitate

Todd and look cool. The sky and water in the background looked pure, blue, and inviting.

Christy stared at the pictures for a long time, reliving the memories they each held.

Paula's card was signed simply, *Thought you might like a copy of these. Aloha and Merry Christmas! Paula.*

Christy wondered how Paula was really doing and guessed from her brief note that she was keeping her life to herself these days.

Christy set the three cards on her dresser where the mementos that reminded her of Todd had been. She decided the pictures only made her think more about Todd, so she pulled the box out from under her bed and added the photos to the collection.

With a heavy sigh, she whispered, "I know I'm not being very cheerful about Your birthday, Jesus. I'll try to think more about You and trust You more to work out all my relationships."

During the two-hour drive up to the mountains on Wednesday, Christy tried extra hard to be nice to her brother. She played a license-plate game with him until the road started to seriously wind, and her stomach felt a little queasy.

"Are we almost there?" David asked. "Where's the snow?"

"These directions indicate we have about a half hour before we reach the Blue Jay turnoff. We should see snow pretty soon," Mom said.

"There's some!" David exclaimed, pointing to a small patch on the side of the hill.

When they arrived at the cabin, the ground was covered with snow, and David was beside himself with glee. He was the first one out of the car. Packing a snowball with his bare hands, he threw it at the windshield and then quickly prepared another one for Dad as he got out of the car.

"Let's take our things in first, David," Dad said. "Looks like Bob and Marti are already here."

Christy stepped inside and gaped at the fully equipped, two-story deluxe home Bob and Marti had rented. It wasn't exactly the log cabin she had envisioned. She should have known. Her wealthy aunt and uncle were accustomed to the finer things in life, which included all the comforts of home wherever they went.

Marti stood on a small stepladder beside the fireplace, gingerly placing Christmas ornaments on a tree that reached to the vaulted ceiling.

"What do you think?" Marti asked, leaning back slightly to admire her handiwork. "It's Santas this year."

Indeed, the entire tree was trimmed in a variety of Santa ornaments. Last year, Christy remembered, it had been lambs. Marti was the only person Christy knew who had a different theme for her Christmas tree every year.

"It's nice," Christy commented. "Are you all done? Do you need any help?"

"I believe I'm finished, dear. Wait until you see it with the lights plugged in. I used red lights this year. Gives the room a wonderful, festive glow."

Dad came in, carrying in a suitcase in each hand, and said, "Christy, could you help your mom bring in the smaller bags? Where do you want us to put all this, Marti?"

Marti descended from her decorator's loft and pointed up the stairs. "I thought you and Margaret would enjoy the morning glory room. It's the second on the right. David is in the daisy room at the far end of the hall, and Christy is next to him in the violet room."

"The rooms have names?" Christy asked, curious to know if the house really came labeled that way or if her aunt's dramatic flair had affected everything in the house.

"Oh, yes! This is a bed-and-breakfast. Bob knows the owners, and they went to London for the holidays. He rented it from them for a song. You'll be favorably impressed with the accommodations, I think. A fireplace in nearly every bedroom!"

"I can't wait to see my room," Christy said.

"Don't forget to help me with the bags," Mom reminded Christy.

Marti added, "Then your mother and I need to make a quick run to the grocery store to stock up on food for the week."

Christy hurried to carry in the bags and waved good-bye as Mom and Marti took off for the store. With anticipation, Christy grabbed her luggage and headed up the stairs to find her violet room.

She decided the first room on the right must be Bob and Marti's. In the center was a four-poster bed with a sheer canopy draped over the top and down the sides. Everything was in red roses and dark cherry wood.

She ventured on down the hall, the thick carpet crushing softly under her feet. The next room turned out to be her parents' morning glory room, with bright blue morning glories painted in a border trailing up the walls. The blue bedspread, rug, towels, and curtains lent the room a cheery look, and Christy knew her mom would like it.

Closing their door, she tiptoed across the hall, feeling as though she were exploring a great castle. The door on the left opened to reveal her violet room. Christy held her breath when she saw it.

It looked like something out of a storybook. In the corner, a fire glowed in the fireplace, and against the wall was a white, wrought-iron daybed with a heart in the center of the back, frosted with a deliciously thick down comforter. Little bunches of violets were everywhere—violets tied with pink ribbon on the wallpaper; pressed violets in small, narrow frames on the night-stand; a soft blanket with embroidered violets over the antique trunk at the end of the bed; and even an oval throw rug by the door with a large clump of violets in the center.

But what captured Christy's heart was the window seat beneath the large double windows. It looked too enchanting to be real. She dropped her bags and approached the seat as if it would run away if she went too fast or startled it. Gently touching the narrow, cushioned seat and fingering the lace on the violet-covered throw pillows, she decided it was indeed real and hers for the next six days.

"Is the room to your liking, miss?" Bob asked, standing in her doorway.

"Oh, you startled me!" Christy said as she turned around. "Yes, it's gorgeous. I love it!"

Just then they heard hoots and hollers outside. Christy leaned her face close to the window and could see David pelting Dad with his meager supply of snowballs. Bob joined Christy in spying on the war about to break out.

"Come on," he said, tagging Christy on the arm. "We can go out the back through the kitchen and ambush them."

"Let me find my gloves." Christy quickly rummaged in her bag and then slipped the gloves on as she galloped down the stairs behind Bob.

Like two secret agent scouts, Bob and Christy crept along the side of the house until they saw Dad and David rapidly tossing snowballs at each other.

"All right, here's the plan," Bob whispered. "We need a fair supply of ammo before we rush them. Let's make a dozen balls each, store them here, and then we'll carry as many others as we can and still throw."

Christy gave her uncle a playful salute and set to work on her dozen snowballs. Next, she and Bob loaded more snowballs in the crooks of their left arms.

"On my signal," Bob said, holding up his right hand and watching for a break in the skirmish between Dad and David. "Okay, now!" he ordered, snapping down his hand and running into the fray, hollering and throwing snowballs as if he were a 10-year-old.

Christy followed right behind him and lobbed her first shot at Dad. He was caught off guard, and the missile hit his right ear. David and Dad's surprise allowed Bob and Christy two more excellent shots before her brother and father retaliated. The battle raged, chilly and full of laughter, as Bob and Christy each took turns returning to the side of the house for ammo.

In a bold move, David cut across their lines, found their secret stash, and used the last few snowballs on them. Bob managed to scoop an armful of snow down David's back before Dad called a truce.

Just then the car containing Marti and Mom turned into the long driveway.

"Quick," Bob said. "Everyone hide, and let's give the ladies a surprise welcome!"

David and Dad scrambled to hide together behind the family car while Bob slipped behind a tree. Not sure where to go, Christy headed for the side of the house but felt sure Mom and Marti had spotted her. She decided to play it cool and act as if she were out for a stroll.

"Hide, Christy!" David yelled in a hoarse whisper as Marti parked the car and turned off the engine.

Mom opened her door and greeted Christy with, "Are you out enjoying the fresh air?"

"Yes," Christy answered, scooping up a handful of clean snow in her gloved hand and licking it like a snow cone.

Marti exited her door, pulled a bag of groceries from the backseat, and said, "Where's Bob?"

Christy hesitated and then decided honesty was always the best policy. "He's hiding in ambush behind that tree over there."

"Christina," Marti scolded, "where do you come up with these things? Do teenagers take smart-answer classes in school these days?"

When Marti was a few feet from her, Christy held out her handful of snow and said, "There's something wrong with this snow. It doesn't smell right."

"What do you mean it doesn't smell right?" Marti asked.

Christy sniffed at the snow mound and said, "I don't know how to explain it, but it doesn't smell like Wisconsin snow."

Mom lugged two sacks of groceries from the backseat and said, "Then, for heaven's sake, don't eat it, Christy. Snow isn't supposed to have any kind of smell."

Christy looked at her aunt with questioning eyes. "What do you think? Does it smell funny to you?"

Marti leaned over, ready to delicately sniff the white stuff. Christy playfully pushed the handful of snow into her unsuspecting aunt's face.

Dad, David, and Bob took that as their signal and sprang from their hiding places, yelling so loudly that Marti dropped her bag of groceries and ran into the house, screaming.

Mom planted her grocery bags in the snow and began to fling a few feeble balls at Dad. David snuck up behind her and shoveled a handful of snow down her jacket.

Letting out a yelp, Mom scooped up snow in both hands and showered the blessing back on David.

Mom, Dad, Bob, and David were all laughing and brushing the snow from their faces when Christy heard Marti calling to her from the window above her. "Oh Christy darling," Marti called. "Up here!"

Christy looked up just in time to see Marti tip a glass of water out the open window. Before Christy could move, the wet bullet found its mark and dripped down her face.

Christy shook off the startling wet surprise and called out, "Okay, okay! We're even, Aunt Marti." Christy waved her surrender at her aunt.

"That's the way I like it," Marti said with a satisfied expression.

Christy went inside to change and met Marti upstairs in the hallway.

"I couldn't resist the opportunity," Marti said with a giggle. "You're a good sport, Christy."

"So are you. You must have been pretty feisty when you were my age."

"Oh, I was!" Marti agreed. "Just ask your mother! Now, put on some dry clothes, and join us downstairs for cocoa."

Marti trotted down the stairs, and Christy thought, *Your poor mother!*

Once Christy was changed and seated at the kitchen counter, she asked, "Do you think we'll be able to do a little shopping somewhere up here today or tomorrow? I need to buy one more present."

She didn't want to mention that the only person she didn't have a gift for was her aunt, the person who had everything.

"The only shopping is at the Lake Arrowhead Village. I don't care to go there tomorrow," Marti said crisply. "It's Christmas Eve day, and the crowds will be unbearable."

"I could take you over," Bob said smoothly. "Or if you like small gift shops, I noticed one about a half mile down the road. I could take you down there, if you'd like."

"I could walk, if it's only a half mile," Christy said, accepting the mug of cocoa Bob held out to her.

"What's only a half mile?" Mom asked, joining them in the kitchen.

"A little gift shop. I still have one more present to get. Is it okay if I walk down there?"

"By yourself?" Mom asked.

"Mom, it's only down the road."

"I suppose it's okay. Thanks, Bob," Mom said, receiving her mug of cocoa. "You'll have to hurry, though. It's already after 2:00. It gets dark faster up here in the mountains, so you would have to be back here before 4:00, I'd say."

"That's fine. I'll leave right now."

"I imagine David will want to go with you," Mom said.

"Mother," Christy said with pleading eyes, "please, may I just go by myself? He's not exactly a gift-shop kind of kid."

"I suppose you're right. Just be careful, okay?"

"I will, Mom. I'll stay on the road; I'll be back by 4:00; and I promise I won't talk to strangers."

Christy hurried to her room to grab her coat and some money.

Bob was waiting for her by the front door. "At the end of our driveway, turn left," he explained. "Then keep heading straight down the road for about a half mile, and you'll see the shop on the right. I think it's called the Alpine Gift Shop. Do you want me to pick you up in an hour?"

Christy was about to turn down his offer, but then she realized the walk there was downhill and would be quick and easy. But the walk back would be all uphill.

"Sure," she said. "My mom will probably feel better about that, won't she?"

Bob smiled. "I'll be there in an hour."

Christy trudged down the driveway before David noticed she was going somewhere. She turned left and kept heading down the cleared street. She was glad for the chance to think and pray, breathing out her prayers in misty puffs of cold air and listening for the answers in the crunch of gravel and ice beneath her feet.

The more she thought and prayed, the more she knew she wanted to be good friends with Rick and get all this tension between them resolved. And she didn't want to be jealous of Katie for having more freedom to do things and for being the center of attention all the time. She wanted Todd back in her life, or more accurately, she wanted to be back in Todd's life. She wanted Todd's arm to be around her, not around his surfboard. And she wanted to feel close to God.

Is it possible to have all these at the same time? Maybe I need to set my priorities in order and reverse the list so God is at the top, with Rick, Katie, and Todd after that.

Into the cold, winter air, she prayed, "I surrender to You, Father. I do this a lot, don't I? I'm glad You don't ever get tired of forgiving me for not trusting You completely. I don't want to run ahead of You. I want to walk with You. I want to hear Your voice and feel Your hand of blessing on my head."

CHAPTER EIGHT

Diamonds in the Sky

Christy found the Alpine Gift Shop right where Bob had said it would be and eagerly entered the warm, fragrant shop. Her nose and ears needed a little thawing out from the cold air.

The small store connected to some kind of big lodge. Christy noticed that soft, Christian praise music was playing in the background.

She began to browse the darling displays of gifts. From the pictures with scriptures on them and from the assortment of T-shirts with Christian messages, she realized the shop must be run by a believer. It made her feel warm inside and at home.

She loved all the frilly, little gift items like the white lace doilies and the stationery trimmed with wildflowers. There was a whole section of books, and an antique trunk bubbled over with stuffed animals.

An elegant white teapot caught her eye. It had a matching creamer and sugar bowl, but she didn't have enough money for the whole set. She also knew it was probably something she would like more than her aunt would.

A collection of angels by the shop's back door gave Christy an idea. She chose an angel Christmas tree ornament that looked as

though it had been made from an old-fashioned lace handker-
chief. Maybe one year Marti would decorate her tree in angels,
and this could be her first one. The price was right, and Christy
felt good about finding something unique and special.

She took the ornament up to the register, and a sweet-smiling
lady with short, blonde, curly hair rang up the purchase. Christy
smiled back, certain that the lady must be a Christian, even
though Christy didn't know what to say to identify herself as one,
too. She thought maybe her smile back could be a secret message
of kinship in Christ.

"Would you like this gift wrapped?" the lady asked.

"Sure, that would be great. Is there an extra charge?"

"No, it's complimentary," the lady said, turning to a tall,
pretty teenager sitting in a chair behind the counter. "Could you
find a box upstairs for this, Amanda?"

The girl had long, blonde hair pulled back in a braid and wore
glasses with light blue frames that Christy thought were flattering
on her. She rose from her cozy spot and walked up the narrow
stairs at the back of the shop.

Christy waited patiently, smiling again at the lady and noticing how much she resembled the teenager. Maybe they were
mother and daughter.

"These are cute angels, aren't they?" the lady commented.
"My mom makes these. She'll be glad to know we sold another
one."

Amanda returned with a box, and the lady carefully laid the
angel inside on a bed of tissue paper.

"Do you want me to get a bow for it, Mom?" the girl asked.

Christy thought how nice it must be for a mother, daughter,
and grandmother to all be involved in running this fun little gift
shop. And if they were Christians, as she suspected, they could

at least say "Merry Christmas" to their customers without being corrected.

Christy thanked the mother and daughter and was about to leave when something inside compelled her to call out, "I hope you have a wonderful celebration of the birth of our God."

Amanda looked at her surprised mother and then back at Christy and said, "Thanks. You, too!"

Bob was waiting in the car for her when she stepped outside, leaving the warm, spicy fragrances locked in the charming little shop. She told Bob how cute the store was and that it was run by a mother and her daughter.

She wondered how Mom, Marti, and she would do if they tried to run a shop together. The more she thought about it, the less pretty the picture became. Mom and Marti were so different; her mom was simple but sturdy, while Marti was all flair and fashion.

Christy especially noticed the differences between Mom and Marti the next night. It was Christmas Eve, and as the whole family ate dinner by candlelight, Dad read the Christmas story from the book of Luke. Bob and Marti respected Christy's family's tradition, although the looks on their faces showed Christy they didn't see the miracle in the story.

Christy smiled, thinking of how Bethlehem must have been filled with Bobs and Martis that night, who hurried about their business, unaware of God's sudden presence among them.

When Dad read about the angel appearing to the shepherds bringing "good tidings of great joy," Christy thought, *A whole city full of important, influential people, and God chose to wake up some lowly shepherds to announce His arrival.*

She glanced at petite, stylish Marti, who seemed poised like a rocket, ready to blast off to the presents under the tree the minute Dad finished reading.

I'd rather be a shepherd, Christy thought, feeling as if she and God had a little secret.

"This one's for Christy," David announced a few minutes later as he scurried around the tree, passing out gifts to the family.

Christy eagerly unwrapped the medium-sized box from her aunt and uncle and discovered a complicated, expensive-looking camera.

"Thanks," she said, not quite sure how to respond to such an unexpected gift.

"Your mom said you signed up for a photography class next semester, and I wanted to make sure you were prepared with the best equipment possible," her uncle explained. "I'll show you how to work it later. It's as easy as can be."

"Thanks," Christy said again.

She didn't know what else to say. The photography class had been almost an afterthought. It had sounded more interesting than some of the other electives offered, and she had been at a loss as to what else to fill her schedule with. Now she had an expensive camera to cement her elective-class decision. Maybe it would help her get a good grade.

"Another one for Aunt Marti," David said, handing Marti a small, long, narrow box tied with a gold ribbon.

"Bob, you shouldn't have," Marti protested. "I told you all I wanted this year was a white Christmas. You already gave me that."

Bob grinned and said in his good-natured way, "I thought you needed a few snowflakes to keep with you all year long."

"Oh, Robert, you are the most wonderful husband in the

world." Marti's long, manicured nails slit the gold ribbon on the box and snapped it open.

With a gasp she exclaimed, "Oh, Robert, it's absolutely beautiful!"

Christy felt as though she were watching a commercial as Marti removed the sparkling diamond bracelet from the box and held it in the light of the red Christmas tree bulbs so everyone could see the glistening bracelet.

Bob looked at Marti proudly, pleased with his wife's reaction. "Am I forgiven for the snowball ambush?" he asked with a grin.

"Yes, yes, a thousand times yes!"

Out of the corner of her eye, Christy caught the expression on her dad's face. Dad was a dairyman, not a self-made real estate millionaire like Uncle Bob. When her parents married, they were so poor that Dad had given her mom a simple gold wedding band. Mom never even had an engagement ring.

How could her mom handle this so graciously? Mom had never received a diamond in her life; yet here she sat, watching her sister ooh and aah over a bracelet filled with diamonds.

Christy's mother leaned over to Dad, placed her hand, the one with the simple gold band on her finger, on his leg and whispered something in his ear. Dad turned and looked at Mom. It was as if they each sent a love letter to the other with their eyes. It was beautiful.

No one else had noticed what had passed between Christy's parents because Bob, Marti, and David were busy trying to close the bracelet's clasp around Marti's slim wrist. Christy felt a little embarrassed, as if she shouldn't have been watching the intimate moment between her parents. At the same time, it made her feel warm and secure.

"Go ahead!" Marti said eagerly. "Someone else open a gift now."

"I will!" David said and dove for the largest box, which did indeed hold the video game set he had been hinting to Uncle Bob for. Another round of squeals and more hugs were lavished on Uncle Bob.

After all the gifts were opened, the wrapping paper crammed into garbage bags, and one last round of cocoa had been poured, everyone headed off to bed.

Christy carried upstairs her new ballet-style slippers and thick, peach-colored robe from Mom and Dad. Bob had already been in her room, and a crackling fire filled the room with its amber glow.

After putting on her pajamas, Christy slipped into the new robe. She felt cozy and surrounded with warmth, ready to stretch out on her window seat.

Tonight no snow fell outside her treetop window. The sky had cleared, and she could see the stars. Tucking her legs under her and pulling the new robe tight around her middle, Christy undid the lock on the double windows and pushed them open.

The brisk night air ran in to greet her. She stuck her head out the open window, gazing up at the stars.

Those stars are Your diamonds, aren't they, God? They're beautiful—like diamonds scattered on black velvet. Why are they scattered? They should be gathered together to fill Your crown, not spilled out on heaven's floor.

For a long time she sat before the open window, watching the stars, breathing in the cold night air, and burrowing her hands in the large pockets of her plush robe. She felt small compared with the vastness before her. All her feelings from the past few days seemed to level out and, in a way, to be insignificant when held up against thoughts of eternity.

When You were a baby, did You see that bright star over Bethlehem? Could You see it from Your manger-bed? Did you know that star was shining for You?

In the stillness, something stirred in Christy's heart, something stronger than she had ever felt before. She felt deeply loved, as if Someone were calling her name without using a voice. It was an invisible communication of love, like her parents using only their eyes to speak to each other.

"I'm here," she whispered back.

That was it. There were no angels, no big celestial experience. Only the stars in the sky and the firm assurance deep within her that God loved her. It was Christmas Eve, and just like the shepherds, Christy felt she'd been included in a great, eternal secret. God is with us!

The next morning, when Christy awoke, she realized it was Christmas, and she was in her charming mountain bedroom. Then she remembered all the warm, close-to-God feelings she had experienced the night before.

She tried to put the feelings into words, as if she were writing a report to document the event. But she couldn't describe it. Besides, no one else needed to know. It was between her and God— something rare and sacred. Last night God had called her by name, and she had echoed back the love.

She could hear someone moving around downstairs and decided to pull on her robe and slippers and join whoever it was. She found Uncle Bob in the kitchen, making breakfast.

"Merry Christmas!" Christy greeted him. "Do you need some help?"

"Sure do, Bright Eyes. The pan on the stove is hot. Can you slide the bacon in there?" Bob asked, placing a tray of homemade cinnamon rolls in the oven.

Within minutes, the cabin filled with the smells of bacon and cinnamon rolls.

"Better start some coffee," Bob advised. "These breakfast smells are sure to rouse the rest of the house in no time. Coffee's over there in the white bag. Can you hand it to me?"

Christy reached for the bag of gourmet coffee and drew in its rich fragrance before handing it to Bob. She loved the smell of coffee but had never liked its taste.

"It's Jesus' birthday," she said suddenly to her uncle.

He had typically slipped out of any conversation she had ever tried to have with him about God. This morning she couldn't help but say something, still feeling God's presence.

Bob didn't respond.

"Did you ever think how amazing it is that God laid down all His power and came to us on our level? He was God, and He let Himself become a baby."

Bob busily measured the freshly ground beans and pressed the coffee maker's "On" button.

"I mean, that kind of love amazes me. To have it all and lay it aside so you can go undercover into enemy territory and rescue the ones you love. That's incredible, isn't it?"

Christy didn't care that her uncle wasn't responding. She was on a roll. God's love seemed so clear to her. "Especially because most of the ones God loved and came to rescue didn't even like Him. But He did it anyway because He loved them. He loves us. He never gives up. He never stops loving us."

Bob turned to face Christy with a tight grin on his face. "You make it sound pretty romantic, young lady."

"I think it is romantic. Jesus is like the ultimate Prince on a white horse coming to the rescue!"

"And I suppose you're the princess."

"Yes," Christy said, holding her head high, "I am. And He saved me."

"What about her?" Bob said, taking several steps into the living room and reaching for a newspaper in the bin of fire-starter material. He held it up so Christy could see a picture of a small girl with huge eyes and a swollen stomach. The newspaper headlines gave statistics of how many had died of starvation that week in the little girl's war-torn country.

"Why didn't your Jesus ride in and save this little princess?" Bob asked.

Christy could feel tears come to her eyes—tears for the little girl and for herself. Bob's question had spoiled the aura of love she had been basking in.

Apparently recognizing how harsh his question had seemed to Christy, Bob tossed the paper down on the hearth and moved close to her.

"Don't get me wrong, Christy. There's your sweet fantasy, and then there's reality. I don't want you to get the two mixed up."

"God isn't a fantasy. His love is more real than anything," Christy stated.

Bob shook his head and gingerly flipped the popping bacon. "If your God is so full of love, then why would He allow that innocent child to suffer?"

Christy drew in a deep breath and answered honestly, "I . . . I don't know."

CHAPTER NINE

Spin Dry

"Let's go!" Dad called out as he carried suitcases to the car for the trip home.

Christy emerged from the cabin carrying a bottle of shampoo and said to Marti, who was already seated in her car, "I found this in your shower."

"Oh, toss it for me, will you? The bottle is wet, and I've already closed my suitcase."

Since the bottle was nearly full of expensive shampoo available only at salons, Christy made sure the lid was on tight and "tossed it" into the trunk of her uncle's car.

Bob carried the last suitcase over and swung it into the car trunk. "That should be it," he said, shaking Dad's hand.

Turning to give Christy a kiss on the cheek, he asked, "When are you going to come up and see us?"

"When do you want me to come?" Christy responded.

"Well, when do you have some time off work?"

"This week. I don't work again until the day after New Year's."

"Is that so?" Bob said, looking back at Christy's dad. "Why don't we take her home with us today? You folks can come up for

New Year's Day, and we'll watch football on my new home-theater system. What do you think, Norm?"

Dad thoughtfully scrunched his eyebrows together. "I don't know, Bob. You sure Marti doesn't mind?"

"Not a bit," Bob said. "We love having you any time. And you know how Marti feels about Christy. She's the daughter Marti never had."

"I suppose it would work out," Dad said. "You'd think we could have discussed this before the last minute when we're ready to leave."

Bob and Dad settled the details as if Christy weren't standing there. Not that she minded them making plans for her, especially since the plans were to go to Newport Beach. The problem was the Rose Parade. She hadn't brought it up with her parents yet, and she needed their permission before she could make any plans with her Newport Beach friends.

"Dad," she said, "I need to ask you something."

Dad looked surprised, as if he had just noticed she was standing there. At that moment Mom joined them.

"Would it be all right with you and Mom if I went to the Rose Parade with Katie and some other friends?"

Dad looked amazed. "When did you dream this up?"

"My friends started to make plans last week, but I was waiting for the right time to ask you."

Bob gave his approval. "Sounds like a great idea! The Rose Parade is a lot of fun for teenagers. They camp out on the street all night. It's quite a tradition with Southern California kids."

"They sleep on the streets?" Mom asked in disbelief.

"Sure. It's fairly safe. Sort of an all-night New Year's Eve party," Bob explained.

Marti, apparently noticing that she was missing out on

something, left her warm spot in the car to join the rest of them.

"Sorry, Christy," Dad said firmly. "Tradition or no, you're not sleeping on the street to watch some parade."

Christy's face showed her full disappointment, and she blurted out, "I knew it. I don't know why I bothered to ask. Katie's going. She went sledding, too. I had to work that day, remember? Katie wanted to go to the Bible study in San Diego at Rick and Doug's, and her parents said it was okay. But I didn't even ask you guys because I knew you'd say no. You always say no." Christy stopped to catch her breath.

"I think she should go," Marti spoke up. "After all, she is 16 and very dependable. And I know most of her friends, and they are all to be trusted. If you're too strict with a child of this age, that child will rebel, you know."

Christy thought her aunt was kind of funny, spouting off her untried child-rearing ideas to Mom and Dad.

Dad looked at Mom, and Mom looked back at him. They seemed to have reached the same conclusion without saying a word to each other.

"We'll compromise on this one, Christy," her dad said, his eyebrows together again, this time with sternness. "You can go to the Rose Parade, but you can't sleep overnight. Either your mother and I will drive you up there early on the morning of the parade, or if Bob wants to, he can drive you."

"No problem," Bob said. "I'd be glad to take her."

"But she'll miss all the fun with the rest of the young people," Marti protested. "The party the night before is what it's all about."

Christy felt like saying, "Hush, Aunt Marti! Let's settle for what we got out of the bargain."

"It's too risky," Mom said. "Maybe when you're a little older, Christy."

"That's fine!" Christy jumped in before Marti had a chance to say anything. "I really appreciate your letting me go. You know it's something I've wanted to do since I was a little kid back in Wisconsin."

"Yes, I know," Dad said. "I'm glad you have the chance to go. Maybe we should plan on all going together as a family next year."

"Oh, Norm," Marti scolded, "what teenager wants to be seen with her parents at a place like that? It's strictly a teen party." Turning to Christy, she added enthusiastically, "Speaking of teen parties, I have the perfect solution. Why don't you invite all your friends to come over to our house after the parade to watch football with your uncle? I'll order some food, and we'll make up for you not being able to sleep over at the parade."

Dad had already lifted Christy's suitcase from the trunk and was walking with it over to Uncle Bob's car.

"We'll call you once we've made our final plans," Marti said to Mom and whisked Christy over to the car. "Bye, all!" Marti called over her shoulder, stepping out of the chill mountain air and into the warm car.

"Now, I thought I'd order one of those deli trays," she continued once they had settled into the car. "Those are always good for a group of hungry young men."

Christy waved good-bye to her parents and watched David appear from the forest, where he had been playing. David pointed at her and looked upset. She imagined he must be whining because she was going with Bob and Marti and he wasn't. Maybe there were some advantages to being the eldest.

Bob steered the car down the narrow, winding mountain road

while Marti rattled on with her big party plans. Christy wondered if the party was really for her or for her aunt.

Two hours later they arrived at Bob and Marti's plush beach-front home, and Christy lugged her suitcase up to her familiar guest room. It was Monday afternoon, and New Year's Eve was three days away.

She had some arrangements of her own to make. First, she would call Katie and let her know she was in Newport and that her parents said she could go to the parade. Then she would call Tracy and see if they could get together over the next few days. Maybe she would call Doug, too. And if she felt really brave, she would call Rick and try to talk things out on the phone so that when she saw him at the parade, things wouldn't be so tense.

Marti had other plans for how Christy would spend the next few days. Before Christy could even unpack her suitcase, Marti was tapping her nails on Christy's door and asking if she could enter.

Armed with a pad of paper and a pen, Marti planted herself on Christy's bed and said, "Let's start the guest list. How many total do you think we'll have, dear?"

"I'm not sure. Maybe six or seven."

"Oh, come on! Certainly you want to invite more than that."

Christy felt she had no way of knowing how many would be there. So she made up a number. "Seventeen."

"All right, then," Marti said, making notes. "Seventeen guests. I'll order the large deli tray and several side salads. Most people like potato salad, don't they?"

"Yes, I'm sure they do."

"Now, for drinks we'll fill the ice chest with sodas and beer."

"Beer?" Christy questioned.

"For the college boys," Marti explained. "They'll want to

drink beer with their potato chips while they watch TV, won't they?"

"Aunt Marti, you know my friends. They don't drink."

"None of them? Not even beer?"

"No! Besides, I would never feel comfortable having a party where alcohol was served. I don't want any beer at this party."

"All right," Marti said, sounding defensive. "I was only trying to help you throw a successful party at which everyone had a good time."

"I know, and I appreciate it. Really. With my friends, though, just getting together is all they need to have a good time."

"You know, Christina," Marti said, putting down the pencil, "you are a unique young lady. I was so different from you when I was your age. In case I haven't told you before, I have great admiration for your strong character. I believe you might make something of yourself."

"Thank you," Christy said. "And thanks, too, for offering to have the party. I appreciate all you do for me."

Looking back at her notepad, Marti pressed on. "Let's see, we'll need lots of snack foods, too. Do you have any preferences? Chips? Candy? We can make a list, and I'll send Bob to the store tomorrow."

The list-making continued for nearly half an hour. Christy was eager to finish so she could make her phone calls.

But as soon as Marti finished with her lists, Bob joined them with a list of his own. "These are the movies playing in town tonight, and the times they start," Bob explained, showing Christy the long list. "If none of them appeals to you, we could rent a video. I also thought we'd go out to dinner, since we're low on groceries. That is, unless you two ladies have already made other plans for the evening."

"No; dinner out would be fine," Marti said. "Why don't you make early reservations at the Five Crowns? I don't think we've taken Christy there yet."

"Okeydokey," Bob said. "Can you two be ready in an hour?"

"Certainly," Marti said. "And Christy, can you separate your laundry? You've probably run out of clean things to wear. Come to think of it, all you have with you are clothes for the mountains. We'll have to go shopping first thing tomorrow morning and buy you something to wear to the Rose Parade and then something to change into for the party."

"I'll call the restaurant," Bob said. "You check out that movie list, Christy, and let me know what you decide."

"I have to change," Marti said, springing up from the bed. "Don't forget those dirty clothes, and try your best to find something nice for tonight. This is a classy restaurant we're taking you to. You might want to shower, if you think you have time."

With that, Marti shut the door, leaving Christy in sudden silence. She sat for a moment, her head still spinning from all the instructions Bob and Marti had dumped on her.

Sometimes I wish my aunt and uncle would get a life and leave mine alone!

Christy gave up on plans to make her calls until tomorrow, realizing that being treated to dinner and a movie was nothing to complain about. She showered and dug through her stuff until she came up with a clean pair of jeans, a knit shirt, and a new vest Aunt Marti had given her for Christmas. She felt proud of herself for coming up with something out of her mound of dirty clothes.

Unfortunately, Marti, dressed in a green silk outfit, didn't share Christy's enthusiasm. "The shirt is all wrong with that vest. I knew I shouldn't have bought just the vest without getting the right kind of cotton shirt to go with it. Is that all you have? It's too casual. I told you this was a nice restaurant."

"I like it," Christy said. "I think it matches this vest you gave me perfectly."

"You both look terrific," Bob said. "If we want to make our 5:00 reservation, we need to leave now."

"You're right," Marti said, backing down. "But we'll take the vest along with us when we shop tomorrow and see if we can't find a better match for it."

Christy decided a smile was the best response. After all, how could she complain about her aunt's generosity?

Besides, she had learned long ago to protest only the big things, like her uncle's declaration that God couldn't be loving if He let that little girl in the newspaper starve to death. Christy was no closer to an answer than she had been on Christmas morning when he had asked her. Yet she knew he was wrong, and someday she would show him why.

In the meantime, it was hard to think of that starving girl and fully enjoy her expensive dinner. Christy felt certain that the amount of money Bob was spending on her dinner tonight would feed someone in another country for a week.

Maybe that was part of the answer she would use on Uncle Bob one day. Maybe God, in His love, had provided an abundance, but people didn't share with those in need, so things became worse until the world ended up as it is today.

Christy liked that answer, although she didn't feel ready to spring it on her uncle.

"Did you decide on a movie?" Bob asked.

"None of the ones on the list looked very interesting," Christy said. "Would it be okay if we rented one instead?"

"Wonderful idea," Marti said. "I'm much more comfortable at home than in a sticky-floored theater. Besides, Bob's new television with the surround-sound system makes our family room even better than a theater."

Marti was right. The effect of the huge screen and the sound coming from all directions was dramatic. Christy had selected one of her favorite movies, and the voices sounded as though they were right behind her. Even though she knew the story by heart, when the movie ended, Christy shuffled off to bed filled with warm, romantic feelings. In her opinion, all movies should leave the viewer with sweet, happy emotions.

The next morning she washed her face, pulled back her hair in a clip and put on the same clothes she had worn the night before. Scooping up her pile of dirty clothes, she headed downstairs.

Just as her foot hit the bottom step, the doorbell rang. She kept heading for the laundry room with her bundle but then realized no one was answering the door. Maybe Bob and Marti weren't up yet.

Retracing her steps, Christy bent her knees, reached for the door knob, and pulled the door open far enough to see who was there. She heard a familiar rippling laugh before she could see over the heap of clothes in her arms. Doug was standing at the door, laughing at her.

"I thought you were the maid," he teased.

"I am, sir," Christy said in a high voice, hiding her face behind the mound of clothes. "Whom do you wish to see, sir?"

Doug cleared his throat. "Would you please inform Mistress Christina that Master Douglas is calling?"

"Yes, sir," Christy said, attempting a curtsy as she stepped backward.

But she didn't realize the hallway rug had bunched up. On her third step back, she lost her footing and slipped. Doug reached out to steady her, but it was too late. Both her arms flew over her head, ejecting all the laundry into the air. Just before she came down hard on her backside, her left foot got caught behind Doug's right leg, causing him to lose his balance and come crashing down on her leg.

Christy let out a shriek and then burst out laughing as all her dirty laundry showered down on them. One of her wool ski socks landed on Doug's head. Christy silently thanked the Lord that a sock, and not her underwear, had crowned him.

"Are you all right?" Doug asked in a gurgle of laughter, rolling his eyes upward to view the sock that was partially hanging down on his forehead.

Christy was laughing so hard she couldn't answer.

"What's going on down there?" Marti called from the top of the stairs.

Bob appeared from the kitchen, a spatula in his hand, asking the same question.

Christy and Doug were both so overcome with laughter, neither of them could speak.

Marti rushed to Christy's side and began to snatch up all the personal articles that had flown in the collision. Doug shook the sock from his head and pulled himself up. He offered Christy a hand to help her up. She was still laughing and felt certain her legs would give way if she tried to stand.

"Just a minute," she said, trying hard to compose herself. She stretched out her arm and took Doug's hand. He drew her up to a standing position and started to laugh all over again.

"What happened here?" Marti wanted to know.

"The doorbell rang, and I had my arms full of laundry," Christy managed to explain before feeling another surge of laughter rising to the surface.

"So, what was all this?" Bob said dryly. "The spin-dry cycle?"

Christy and Doug looked at each other and burst out laughing again.

"Honestly," Marti muttered, gathering up the rest of the clothes and marching off to the laundry room with her arms full.

"When you two can see straight again, I have some scrambled eggs ready," Bob said, lifting his spatula into the air and charging back into the kitchen.

Christy caught her breath. Wiping the laughter tears from her eyes, she asked Doug in her pretend maid voice, "Would you care for some breakfast, sir?"

"Sure," Doug said. "On one condition."

"What's that?"

He bent his knees, and before Christy realized what was happening, he placed one strong arm across her back and the other under her knees, scooped her up, and carried her toward the kitchen. "You let me do all the walking this time."

CHAPTER TEN

Just Friends

"How did you know I was here?" Christy asked Doug once she was safely seated in her chair at the kitchen table.

"I called your house last night. Your mom told me. She also told me you're going to the Rose Parade with us."

"To the parade, yes. Overnight, no."

"How are you getting up to Pasadena?" Doug asked.

"My favorite chef is taking me," Christy said as her uncle scooped a small portion of scrambled eggs onto her plate and popped two sausages next to it. "Oh, Bob? Have you met Doug? Doug, this is my Uncle Bob."

Doug extended his hand to shake Bob's, but Bob had a frying pan in one hand and a spatula in the other.

"Nice to meet you, Doug. Say when." Bob began to shovel eggs onto Doug's plate.

Christy watched as the plate became nearly covered with the mound before he said, "That looks great. Thanks."

"Do six of these sausages sound like a good start for you?" Bob asked. "I can make more. I have toast coming, too."

"Sounds great. I sure appreciate this." Doug sprinkled pepper over his eggs.

"You know," Doug said to Christy, "I was thinking of driving up to Pasadena early that morning. You could come with me, if you wanted to. I mean, if your uncle doesn't mind."

"You can call me Bob," he said, placing a plate of toast before them. "And no, I don't mind. It's up to Christy."

She looked at her uncle and then back at Doug. "You really weren't planning on going up that morning, were you, Doug? You wanted to sleep over ever since we started talking about this."

"I've done the sleep-over part before. It's all right. It gets cold, though; you don't sleep at all; and the junk food only gives you a buzz for about the first four hours. By the time the parade starts, everyone is kind of burned out. I'd much rather drive up that morning. We can start early, stop along the way for breakfast, and then join our cranky, hungry friends. What do you think?"

"I know you're doing this to be nice, Doug."

"Okay, so I'm nice. Do you want to go with me?"

"Sure," Christy finally agreed. "I'll have to ask my parents to make sure it's all right with them."

Doug smiled and shoveled another forkful of eggs into his mouth. Christy glanced at her uncle. He winked at her, and she knew the matchmaker wheels were spinning in his head. It reminded her of Jon and the fortune cookie that said she didn't know what she had before her.

Could it be that Doug actually was interested in her as more than a friend? She wasn't sure she was ready to process that thought.

Marti made her grand appearance with her hair done and her makeup on. Christy introduced the two, and Marti said, "I'm sure I've seen you around before. Weren't you the one who stopped by in the yellow truck last year right after Christy and I returned from the hair salon?"

Boy, Aunt Marti, you should consider volunteering for the FBI! I'd forgotten all about that. You don't miss a thing, do you?

"Could have been me," Doug said. It obviously wasn't a monumental memory to him.

Christy remembered it because she had just come from the hair salon and she and Doug were standing in the front yard talking. Doug had said her hair smelled like apples and leaned over to smell it just as Todd drove by. Christy had felt certain Todd had seen her with Doug in their awkwardly close position.

Things sure change in a year. I was so embarrassed then. But this morning Doug falls all over me, and I think it's funny. Have I changed? Has Doug? What's different?

Christy remembered one other incident that happened that day a year ago. That's when Doug told her he was going to take Tracy out. Even though nothing seemed to come of their dating, Christy had noticed when they went out to pizza after the sledding that Doug and Tracy still acted like close friends. That's the way Christy wanted to be with Rick.

Christy decided that as soon as she could break free from Aunt Marti's schedule, she would see Tracy and ask her how she had managed to remain such good friends with Doug.

"I thought we'd go shopping first thing, Christy," Marti stated. "And Bob, I have a grocery list all ready for the party, and—oh, Doug, how rude of me!"

"What?" Doug asked. "Do you have a chore on your list for me, too?"

"Of course not! I nearly forgot to invite you to my party. I mean, to Christy's party. We're having a party for Christy on New Year's Day right after the Rose Parade. I do hope you'll be able to come."

"Sure. Sounds great," Doug said.

"All your friends are invited, and we'll have lots of food."

"And football on my new TV," Bob added.

"Count me in," Doug said, finishing his last crumb of toast. Christy couldn't believe he had eaten everything set before him.

"Wonderful," Marti said, reaching for her notepad on the counter. "That's one I can check off my guest list. Or rather, Christy's guest list."

Get a life, Aunt Martha!

"Sounds as though all of you have a busy day planned. I don't mean to hold you up," Doug said, scooting back his chair. "I did want to ask you, though, Christy, if you don't already have plans for tonight, do you want to have dinner with me over at Tracy's house?"

For a minute Christy thought he was asking her out to dinner, and she started to feel panicked, not knowing how to answer.

"Are you sure it's okay with Tracy and her mom?" Christy asked when she realized the offer was to go to Tracy's house.

"Of course. I told Tracy last night that you were here, and she asked me to invite you."

"I'd like to see her," Christy said. "If you're sure it's okay, then yes, I'd like to come."

"Great! Why don't I pick you up around 5:45?"

"Do you mean pick her up in your car or pick her up the way you delivered her to the breakfast table?" Bob asked with a mischievous twinkle in his eye.

Doug pushed himself back from the table and smiled down at Christy. "Whatever it takes," he said. "Preferably just in my truck."

Christy started to rise from the table. Doug put out his hand to stop her.

"Please," he said, "don't bother seeing me to the door. I'd like to make my exit a little less eventful than my entrance."

Christy smiled back and said, "As you wish, sir."

"Thanks again for the breakfast," Doug said, waving to Bob and Marti. Pointing at Christy, he said, "I'll see you tonight." Bob and Marti looked at Christy with knowing grins as they listened to Doug walk toward the front door.

The minute Christy heard the door close, she blurted out, "I know what you're both thinking, and you can stop right now!"

Bob and Marti exchanged innocent looks and playfully shrugged their shoulders.

"He's just Doug. We're just friends. He's being nice to me, that's all. Stop looking at me like that!"

Bob silently cleared the table. Marti scribbled something on one of her notes. Looking up with a straight face, she said, "Shall we go shopping, then?"

Christy obediently followed her aunt's schedule, waiting all day for Marti to say something about Doug. To Marti's credit, she didn't say a word.

They shopped for four hours, and Christy picked out two outfits, both on sale. They came home, and she finished her laundry and straightened up the guest room. Still Marti said nothing. Bob coaxed Christy into a short walk on the beach later in the afternoon. She felt certain he would have some words of wisdom regarding Doug. But, no. Bob was silent, too.

She actually felt relieved when Doug showed up. Now she could stop constructing explanations in her mind.

Doug opened the truck door for her, and she climbed in. The feeling of being free to come and go under Bob and Marti's unrestrictive care was something Christy always enjoyed. It always felt like a little vacation from the more confining rules of her parents at home.

Some letters lay on the driver's seat, and Christy picked them up so Doug could get in without sitting on them.

"Anything exciting in your mail today?" she asked.

She really wanted to ask if Todd had ever written to him, but she knew it wasn't likely.

"Sorry about that," Doug said, taking the mail from her and sticking it in the side pocket on the inside of his door.

Then, pulling one letter out, he said, "As a matter of fact, yes. I received a letter today from Joab."

Doug handed her a piece of unusual, brownish paper with tiny scribbled words written in pencil. It was hard to read.

"Who's Joab?" Christy asked as Doug started up the truck.

"He's a kid from Kenya. Here, I have his picture in my wallet." Doug opened the glove compartment, took out his wallet, and showed Christy a picture of a thin African boy about 10 years old. He had a serious expression on his face and was wearing what looked like a school uniform.

"How did you meet him?" Christy wanted to know. She recognized the look in Joab's eyes. It was the same haunting look of the starving girl in the newspaper. Only Joab looked much healthier.

"Our God-Lovers group started to sponsor him when school started. We put this big mayonnaise jar by the front door at our apartment, and everyone drops in pocket change. After about a month, I rolled all the coins, and we had almost 30 bucks, which was more than it costs to feed Joab for a month. Isn't he a cool kid?"

"Doug, that is so neat! I want to do that. How did you sign up for a kid?"

"A bunch of good organizations out there offer sponsorships. Here," he said, reaching for the empty envelope Joab's letter came in. "You can have this. It has the address on the front."

Christy folded the envelope and tucked it in her back pocket. This was a way she could give back some of what God had blessed her with. Maybe she could even talk Bob and Marti into sponsoring a child. Why only one child? Bob could finance a whole orphanage.

Tracy's mom had made lasagna for dinner. When Doug took a fourth helping, Tracy poked Christy under the table, and they exchanged expressions of amazement.

After dinner, Tracy's dad and Doug went out to "shoot hoops." Her mom said she would take care of the dishes, so Tracy and Christy retreated to Tracy's room.

"Where does he put it?" Christy asked. "And how could he possibly go outside and run around after eating like that?"

"I know," Tracy said, giggling. "One time last year Doug and I went out to dinner, and I was so embarrassed because he kept asking the waiter to fill the bread basket. I think Doug must have eaten two loaves of bread plus a huge dinner."

"How long did you guys date?" Christy asked. "I mean, how long were you officially going together?"

"I don't know that we ever went together. It was . . . well, you remember; you were here then. We kind of went out for about two months—maybe less. It was really silly."

"That's about how long I went out with Rick. But he and I are barely speaking to each other now. How did you and Doug manage to keep your friendship?"

Tracy looked confused. "We were friends for a long time before I developed those crazy ideas about needing him to be my boyfriend. I don't know. The dating part was the strained part. The friend part has always been easy with Doug."

"It's not that way with Rick. With him, it's all or nothing.

And right now it's nothing.'' Christy lay across Tracy's bed on her stomach, dangling her head and arms over the edge.

"I take it you two didn't talk the other night after pizza," Tracy said.

"No, I really blew it. I called him Todd."

"You called Rick, Todd?"

"Well, he was coming on strong, pressuring me and saying I didn't trust him. I was thinking that Todd would never treat me like that, and then I slipped and called him Todd."

Tracy rolled over on her back and was silent for a moment before saying, "May I ask you a personal question? You don't have to answer if you don't want to."

"What?"

"Did you ever kiss Rick?" Tracy asked.

"Yeah, a bunch of times. Or, I guess if you want to be more accurate, he kissed me a bunch of times. We didn't do anything more than that, in case that's what you're wondering. Why? Didn't you and Doug kiss when you were dating?"

"No."

"No? You dated almost two months, and he never kissed you?"

"Doug has never kissed any girl."

"You're kidding! How old is he?"

"He turned 20 last month. Didn't you know that about Doug? The first girl he wants to kiss is his wife, and their first kiss will be at the altar on their wedding day."

"Really? I never knew that."

"I thought he and Todd had made some monk pact and that you knew about it." Tracy suddenly sprang to an upright position. "Wait a minute. Do you mean to tell me that Todd has actually kissed you?"

Christy sat up, too, feeling a little self-conscious. "Only four or five times, always in front of other people."

Tracy looked at Christy with a glimmer in her eye. "I'm surprised. That really means something, Christy. I'm sure you're the only girl Todd has ever kissed."

The feeling of being special diminished when Christy realized Todd wasn't the only guy she had kissed. That moment she wished she had never dated Rick Doyle. She wished she could have the last few months to do all over again, knowing that she would do things a lot differently. Neither Rick nor any other guy would pressure her into being anything other than who she truly was from the heart out.

"Don't look so serious," Tracy said. "Hey, you know what they say, don't you? Sometimes you have to kiss a couple of toads before the handsome prince comes along."

CHAPTER ELEVEN

The White Rose Parade

When Doug arrived at 5:00 on New Year's morning, Christy answered the door ready to go, with a blanket in one hand and a bag of cookies in the other.

She couldn't help but look at him differently than she had in years past. Doug had to be the only 20-year-old guy in the world who fed starving children and was totally saving himself for his future wife. That kind of godliness was, as Doug had said, irresistible.

"My carriage awaits you, Princess," Doug said, playfully bowing at the front door.

"I'm leaving now," Christy called upstairs into the early morning stillness.

"Hold on," Bob called back from the kitchen. He emerged with a picnic basket bulging with the breakfast he had prepared for them. "I didn't know if you would find many restaurants open on a holiday. So I thought this might hold you over until you can find some real food."

"Thanks," Christy said.

"Thanks," Doug echoed, reaching for the basket.

"We'll see you and your gang after the parade," Bob said. "Have a good time!"

Christy waved good-bye and followed Doug to his truck. He had left the engine running and the heater on, so it was nice and warm inside. The hour or so drive to Pasadena turned into a picnic adventure. Christy kept Doug supplied with a steady stream of blueberry muffins and held his carton of orange juice so he could drink it without taking his hands off the wheel or his eyes off the road. Bob had provided a bountiful feast, and Doug, true to form, put it all away.

"I told my uncle about Joab," Christy said. "And I gave him the address and told him I was going to sponsor a child. I also told him I thought he should sponsor a few kids."

"How did he take that?" Doug asked.

"Pretty well, I think. He didn't say much. See, over Christmas we had this discussion about how could God be loving when starving people are in the world. I told him yesterday that I thought God had given him enough money to help do something about starvation, but he had to be willing to share his wealth."

"Whoa, Christy! Harsh attack, don't you think?"

"I felt strongly about it, and I wanted Uncle Bob to see that I was serious. I've always felt free to tell him whatever I think."

Doug flashed a smile at her and said, "I think you're right about sharing our money. But it's hard to think like Job in the Bible and say, 'The Lord gives, and the Lord takes away. Blessed be the name of the Lord.'"

Christy thought a minute and said, "Job was that guy in the Bible with all the trials, right?"

"Right," Doug said. "He lost everything, but he still hung tough and didn't blame God for his problems. In the end God blessed him over and above what he had before all the bad stuff happened."

"I don't know if I could have that much faith," Christy admitted.

"I know I couldn't," Doug said. "And God knows it, too, because He hasn't done to me what He did to Job. God seems to have a measuring cup for each person and only measures out the dosage that's right. Pretty awesome, huh?"

"Do you think God really measures out a huge dosage to starving children, and do you really think they can handle it?" Christy asked, not convinced by Doug's answers.

"I don't know," Doug said, turning off the freeway. "I do know that He knows each one of them by name, and He promises to provide for everything He created. I also know that we're spoiled rotten, and we don't even know it. We expect God to be our own personal slave and bring us whatever we want whenever we ring the prayer bell.

"It's supposed to be the other way around," Doug continued. "He's God. He's awesome. He can do whatever He wants. He's the Master. We're the ones who are supposed to be the servants— His servants."

Christy knew she had fallen into the spoiled-rotten category more than once. She knew she had treated God that way before, like her personal slave.

"So, how does a person become a servant of God?" she asked.

"By surrendering. Offering yourself to Him."

"I seem to have to do that over and over," Christy admitted.

"Oh, me too," Doug agreed. "It's a constant thing. We have to keep choosing if we'll serve God or ourselves. It's usually easier to serve ourselves."

"I'm just glad He doesn't keep track of how many times I ask

Him for forgiveness," Christy said.

Doug smiled. "I know what you mean. God is pretty awesome, isn't He?"

Christy agreed, and looking out her window at all the parked cars lining the streets, she added, "I really appreciate your driving me up here today, Doug."

Her emotions had begun to flirt with the idea of what it would be like to go out with Doug like this on a regular basis. He was a special guy. After all, Bob, Marti, and even Jon seemed to think she should recognize what a treasure he was.

"I'm glad it worked out. You're like a little sister to me, Christy, and I enjoy keeping an eye on you for Todd." Doug glanced at her as if he weren't supposed to have said that.

Christy felt disappointed and not quite sure if she should feel insulted. It was embarrassing to have romantic thoughts about someone who saw himself as her bodyguard.

"Can I ask you something?" Christy asked, speaking fast before she lost her courage. "Are you interested in being with me because I'm your friend, or did Todd make you promise that you would guard me or something while he was gone?"

"What I said sounded kind of rude, didn't it?"

"I'm not sure what you were trying to say," Christy said.

"I like spending time with you, Christy, and I think you're a really awesome sister in the Lord. But I would never think of seriously dating you as long as that bracelet is on your wrist. Todd's my closest friend, and I'd never snake him."

Christy glanced down at the gold chain on her wrist and realized it was the one part of Todd she hadn't buried in the box with the rest of her souvenirs during her memorial service. She was so used to wearing it that she hadn't even thought to take it off.

"But did Todd put me up to this? No. I want to spend time with you because you're you and I value our friendship. I'm not much into dating, anyway. Tracy probably told you I'm much better at being friends."

Christy appreciated Doug's honesty, and she knew they were both better off keeping their relationship just the way it was. Still, she couldn't help but wonder if anything would be different between her and Doug if Todd hadn't found his way into her heart.

She had met Doug and Todd the same day. What was it that made her and Todd close while it left her and Doug "just friends"?

"Oh, good!" Doug said. "There's a spot for us to park over there."

He pulled the truck onto a dirt area alongside dozens of other cars and turned off the engine. He and Christy loaded their arms with blankets, a small ice chest, and of course, the bag of cookies they had been saving.

They walked for several blocks until they came to Colorado Boulevard, where hundreds of people lined the streets, huddling in beach chairs with their sleeping bags pulled up to their chins. On one corner they passed a portable outhouse with a short line of people waiting to use it.

Christy noticed an older house with a wide front porch and a huge tree in the front yard. A hammock hung between the porch and tree, and two boys around her brother's age were wedged together in the hammock, covered with blankets and looking like a big cocoon suspended in the moist morning air.

Uncle Bob was right. Everyone sleeps outside waiting for the parade. If my parents could see this, they would know it would have been harmless for me to have done it, too.

A few yards up, Christy noticed some college-age guys tossing a Nerf football in the blocked-off street.

"That looks like Rick," Christy said. "I don't know who that guy with him is, though."

The guy receiving Rick's pass had on a navy blue sweatshirt with the hood pulled over his head, which made it difficult to determine his identity.

"You don't suppose . . . ," Doug began and then stopped.

"What?" Christy asked.

"Oh, it's crazy," Doug said. "For a minute I thought the guy over there with Rick might be Todd. Todd always wears a sweatshirt like that."

Christy felt an immediate rush inside as if she had just taken a dip on a roller coaster with her eyes closed. *It can't be Todd. Can it? What if it is?*

"Hey, Rick!" Doug called out, waving.

Rick held the football and looked around.

"Over here," Doug yelled.

Rick spotted him and waved back. The other guy jogged over with him, and Christy eagerly tried to see who it was. He didn't run like Todd.

The guy pulled down the hood of his sweatshirt and revealed flaming red hair that could only belong to Katie.

"Hi!" Katie greeted them enthusiastically.

Christy drew in a deep breath and felt her stomach do another dive.

"Where did you get that sweatshirt?" she snapped at Katie.

"It's my brother's. Why?"

"Oh, I just wondered," Christy said, trying to calm down. "So, where's everybody else?"

"We never found them last night," Katie said.

"You mean you and Rick stayed here all night, just the two of you?" As soon as she said it, Christy realized how accusing she sounded.

"Boy, what's with you this morning?" Katie asked. "Get up on the wrong side of the new year?"

"No, I'm sorry. Take back everything I said. Let's start over." Christy changed her voice to a brighter tone. "Oh, Katie, hi! I'm glad we found you. How's it going?"

Katie gave Christy a questioning look and said, "Rick wanted to wait until you guys arrived before we went looking for the rest of the group, since this is the street corner Doug told him to wait on."

Rick and Doug, their arms loaded with Rick's and Katie's stuff, joined the two girls. Rick handed Katie her backpack and blanket.

"Ready to go on safari?" Doug asked. "The rest of the group has to be around here somewhere."

Feeling like a refugee, Christy fell in step behind Doug, and Katie did the same behind Rick. The guys led them out into the street, where it was much easier to walk without obstacles.

"I feel that people are looking at us as if we're part of the parade," Christy said to Katie. "I hope we find the rest of the group soon. This stuff is getting heavy."

"Look over there," Katie said, pointing across the street to a guy setting up a television camera on an adjustable metal platform.

"Hi, Mom," Katie called out, waving to the camera. "Happy New Year!"

Then, liking the idea of being in the middle of the parade route much more than Christy did, Katie started to goof off, waving to the little kids who lined the curbs.

"Good morning, little friends!" she said in her elf voice. "Rise and shine. The big parade is coming soon!"

"Stop it," Christy said in a mock scold. "They're starting to wave at you. They think you're part of the parade."

Katie laughed and waved back. "You've got to take your fans where you can find them!"

Then they heard someone calling, "Hey, Christy, Doug! Over here."

The foursome crossed the street as they spotted Heather and Tracy standing and waving at them. A group of about a dozen people Christy knew from previous beach gatherings was camped out beside the street. For the next 10 minutes, there was a flurry of hugs, introductions, and explanations.

Once they settled in and wedged their blankets into the space available, Christy plopped herself down next to Tracy and said, "I feel like a pioneer woman who just made a six-month trek to California. Somehow this whole Rose Parade was a lot more glamorous from the comfort of my living room couch."

"So?" Tracy asked. "Did you talk to Rick yet?"

Before Christy could answer, Rick, who they didn't realize was standing behind them, stuck his head between them and asked, "Did I hear someone mention my name?"

"Oh!" Tracy said, startled.

She looked at Christy and then at Rick and said, "I was asking Christy if you two had a chance to talk yet."

Christy turned her head away from Rick.

"I don't know," Rick said. "Have we had our talk yet, Christy?"

"Not exactly," she said, still not looking at him.

"Then maybe you'd better step into my office," Rick said, offering his hand to pull her up.

Christy let him help her to her feet and gave Tracy a grimace that said, "Why did you say anything?"

Tracy smiled and blew Christy a kiss to send her on her way.

Rick led Christy away from the crowd and headed down a street that crossed the parade route. He stopped at a low cement-block fence that edged the front of someone's yard. Sitting down, he motioned for Christy to sit beside him.

She remembered the time last year when Rick sat with her on a cement-block wall at school and talked her into trying out for cheerleader. Today the damp chill from the cold cement shot right through Christy's jeans, and she shivered.

"Cold?" Rick asked, pulling off his high school letterman's jacket and wrapping it around her shoulders before she could answer.

The jacket smelled like Rick. It felt like Rick's arms were once again around her. He was being so sweet and looked at her so tenderly. This was finally their moment to talk, and she had absolutely no idea what it was she wanted to say to him.

"You know, you're the only girl I've ever done this with," Rick said, a half grin pulling up the side of his mouth.

"Done what?" Christy asked.

"I've never talked to any of the girls I've dated after we broke up. You're the first one. Their friends would talk to me sometimes. Usually it was only to tell me what a jerk I was to their friend."

This was a vulnerable side of Rick she knew he didn't show often. Christy used her eyes to tell Rick to continue.

"Ever since junior high," he explained, "I'd go out with a girl, break up with her, and never talk to her again. Now that I'm in college, I have a bunch of girls who are good friends. And, you see, you're in the middle. You're not like any of the girls I dated in high school, and you're not one of the girls from our college

Bible study. I don't really know what to do with you."

With Rick's jacket warming her and everything so tender between them, Christy wanted to say, "Take me in your arms and hold me. I'll be whatever you want me to be, Rick!" Fortunately, she remembered all the strained feelings, hurts, and insecurities from when they had dated. She remembered Rick's arrogant nerve when he took Todd's bracelet from her.

"Let me be one of your friends, like the girls at your Bible study," Christy said softly. "I want to be friends with you the way I am with Doug and these others. And I want you to be friends with Tracy, Heather, and Katie. I want us to all do things together and not have to feel weird because of what went on in the past."

"I want that, too," Rick said, reaching over and squeezing her hand. "Friends?"

"Friends," Christy agreed, squeezing his hand back. "Are you sure we're okay?" she asked as an afterthought.

"What do you mean?" Rick asked.

"The last time we tried to talk, you said that you didn't think I trusted you and that I'd never given our relationship a chance. Do you still feel that way?"

Rick let out a deep breath. "I guess it's no secret that I've always felt a little jealous of the place Todd has in your life. Maybe there's room for both of us. Maybe there isn't. You're going to have to be the one to decide. I don't see any harm in you and me being friends and you and Todd being friends, as long as that's what we all are. Friends."

Christy thought she liked the arrangement, even though something in Rick's voice made her wonder if he didn't want more from their relationship. For now, though, Rick seemed willing to wait and be friends, and that's what she had wanted from him.

She had a hard time believing this was the same Rick who had dumped her in the mall parking lot a week ago. Whatever it was that had softened him, Christy was grateful for it and felt more relieved than she had imagined she would feel. Finally she could fully surrender this relationship to the Lord.

A vendor was heading for the parade route, carrying a flat of roses.

"We'll take one of those," Rick called out to the guy. "How much?"

"Five dollars each," the man said, displaying his assortment of colored rosebuds.

Rick pulled a crumpled five-dollar bill from his pocket and said, "Give me a red one."

"Red is for love," the man said with a satisfied grin, taking the bill and handing the rosebud to Rick. Christy remembered all the red roses Rick had given her while they were dating. Once they had died, she had thrown them all away.

Rick looked at Christy and then back at the assortment of buds. "Which one stands for friendship?"

The man reached for a yellow rose. "Yellow," he said, trading the yellow bud for the red one in Rick's hand.

"What's white for?" Rick asked.

The man didn't seem to mind all the questions. "Purity of heart," he said.

"We'll take the white one," Rick said.

As soon as the vendor was on his way, Rick turned to Christy and said, "You're the first girl I've ever given a white rose to. Did you hear what he said? It stands for purity of heart, and that's you, Killer Eyes."

Christy accepted the white rose, swallowing a lump in her throat. It was the highest compliment Rick had ever paid her. This rose she knew she would keep.

CHAPTER TWELVE

Katie, You Didn't!

When Christy and Rick joined the rest of the group, Doug noticed them first. Holding out the bag of cookies Christy had made for him, he said, "Rick, you have to try these. They're the best ones yet!"

Tracy came alongside Christy and said, "So? How did it go?"

"Good," Christy whispered back. "I think everything is finally settled, and I feel good about it."

"That's what I wanted to hear," Tracy said. "Sorry if I kind of forced you into it."

"I'm glad you did," Christy admitted. "I don't think I would have talked to him otherwise. You did the right thing, Tracy. Thanks." Tracy was staring at the white rose in Christy's hand, and so Christy added, "Rick gave it to me. A gift of friendship."

Tracy smiled. "I'm glad that's settled. It's a good way to start the new year."

For the next hour, the group ate and talked, and the guys and Katie played more football out in the street. More and more vendors appeared, selling souvenirs.

Christy was content to sit on her blanket and watch the action going on around her. The morning warmed up quickly, and she shed her thick jacket.

Then official Rose Parade guards walked briskly along the street, shooing everyone back up on the curb. People began to press in closer, crowding Christy and Tracy together on their blanket. The spectators stretched their necks to see what was coming up the street.

They heard sirens. A group of motorcycle cops led the parade's way; then the official white Rose Parade convertibles with dignitaries waving from the backseats rolled by.

"Who is *he?*" Christy asked when the first convertible passed them.

"Who knows," Tracy said. "Somebody important. Just wave at him."

Tracy and Christy laughed and waved, like two little kids sitting on the curb. The important person waved back.

The Marine Corps Color Guard and Band followed the cars and started to play just as they marched past Christy and the group. It was so loud she wanted to cover her ears with her hands but refrained, since no one else was. The drums seemed to shake the ground and make her heart thump. She had been to parades before, but nothing like this.

The first float that came by amazed Christy. It was a huge, green dragon with steam coming from its nostrils. The monster swerved down the street and came within a few feet of Christy. She could see up close all the layers of flowers carefully placed on the float's frame. The variety of colors and types of flowers was astonishing. The dragon's scales seemed real.

"Look," Tracy said, laughing as she pointed at the dragon's legs. "Those are brussels sprouts!"

"You're kidding!" Christy responded.

"They really are. And look, they used brussels sprouts on the tail, too! It's a vegetarian dragon!"

The group around Tracy and Christy laughed.

Doug, who was sitting on the other side of Tracy, said, "I give it an eight." He held up eight fingers and whistled.

Rick picked up on Doug's cue and held up eight fingers from his spot at the far end of their clump of friends. Christy noticed that Katie had planted herself in front of Rick's lawn chair, using his legs for a backrest. They looked awfully comfortable sitting together.

The next float appeared, and Doug and Rick, wearing matching sunglasses, slipped their glasses down their noses and looked at each other as if they were two official parade critics. Rick held up five fingers as the float motored by, and Doug gave it a six.

"That float deserves more than a five or a six!" Christy exclaimed to Tracy.

The float resembled a field of grass with giant wildflowers and a huge storybook spread open in the middle of the field. Animated butterflies escaped from the storybook, and a wobbly rainbow arched over the field, raining down colored glitter on the parade spectators.

"I give it a nine and a half," Christy said, holding up to Doug nine fingers and half a pinkie.

"Naw," Doug said. "It's only a six. Wait until one of the award-winning floats comes by. You'll see."

As soon as the next float arrived, Christy held up seven fingers, to which Katie responded over the heads of their friends with a three. Rick gave it a four and Doug a five.

"Come on, you guys," Christy said. "That was a good one!"

"I'd give it a seven, too," Tracy said.

"Well, I don't see your fingers up there," Christy teased.

Tracy stuck seven fingers up in Christy's face. "There!" she said.

A band from a Minnesota high school came by, and Rick started to whistle loudly, trying to get the attention of one of the girls playing a flute in the front row.

"That guy doesn't ever take a break, does he?" Tracy said, speaking loudly over the music.

Christy shook her head in response. "I suppose I shouldn't turn my back on him. That's what my boss, Jon, says." Christy and Tracy were speaking so loudly that Doug heard them.

"You should have seen Rick last semester with this girl who lived in our apartment complex. He never let up on her, and she told him to get lost in at least four different languages."

Tracy looked at Christy for her reaction. Christy carefully kept a straight face, looking at Doug as if she were interested in his amusing little story and eager for him to continue.

Doug started to laugh at some funny memory he had. Leaning closer to Tracy and Christy, he let them in on the joke. "Rick used to know when she did her laundry. I think she did it every Tuesday afternoon or something. Anyway, he would go down to the laundry room with a basket full of dirty clothes and wait for her, pretending he happened to be there folding clothes. He would come back to the apartment with neatly folded dirty clothes."

"And she never went out with him?" Tracy asked.

"She didn't even tell him her name!" Doug said, laughing. "The guy can't handle being shut out."

"Hey," Rick called over to them, "let's see those scores!" Rick was holding up a seven, and Katie had five fingers up in the air. The rest of the group had all joined in and were holding up their scores. Doug quickly checked out the float in front of them and gave it a six.

Christy didn't feel like playing anymore. Of course she knew when Rick went to college last fall he would meet girls and probably be his flirty self. But the first two months of school she was dating him. She felt sick in the pit of her stomach, thinking that while he was taking her to the beach on the weekends, he was chasing girls in the laundry room during the weekdays.

"Hey," Tracy said, giving her a poke in the side, "are you okay?"

Christy nodded, but apparently Tracy could see right through her. "Don't let what Doug said about Rick bug you. You and Rick are friends now, remember? Don't let any bad feelings start up again."

"I was thinking that the girl in the laundry room was smarter than I was. She didn't fall for Rick's tricks. I feel foolish, that's all."

"Why?" Tracy wanted to know. "Because you liked a guy and went out with him a few times? I don't see any harm in that. You guys are friends now. There's nothing foolish about any of that."

"I feel like a fool because I believed everything Rick said. Why should I even believe what he told me this morning? Why did I so eagerly accept this rose from him?"

"You have to start somewhere," Tracy said, slipping her arm around Christy and giving her a quick hug. "Don't make such a big deal out of it. Oh, look at this float; a definite 10!" Tracy held up all 10 fingers and whistled wildly with the others.

Tracy's right. I shouldn't make such a big deal out of everything. What Rick does or who he goes out with is no concern of mine.

By the time the next float approached, Christy had joined back in with the rest of the group in playing the rating game. Another band followed and then a float that turned out to be Christy's favorite.

Cinderella rode in an enchanted pumpkin carriage drawn by real horses. The carriage was completely done in roses and smelled wonderful as it passed by. It was a small float, it hadn't won any awards, and the Cinderella looked as though she had been smiling and waving for too many miles.

Rick gave it a one; Katie a two; Doug and Tracy gave it a three and then slapped each other a high five for coming up with the same number.

Christy didn't hold up her hands at first. Then realizing that she was among friends and she should be free to express her opinion, she held up a perfect 10, thereby declaring to them all that she believed in fairy tales.

Rick noticed and, thinking it was a joke, joined in with Christy's 10, raising both his hands high over his head, standing up and whistling to get Cinderella's attention. The model in the float didn't pay any attention to Rick, and Christy tried to tell herself she shouldn't either.

She really did think it was a 10. So what if Rick made fun of her? What did he know about fairy tales, anyway?

After the Cinderella float, there was a lag in the parade. Someone behind them said there must have been a breakdown in one of the floats.

"Perfect opportunity to visit the little girl's room," Tracy said, rising to her feet. "Want to come with me?"

Christy stood and instructed Doug, "Save our places. Don't let anyone sit here, okay?"

Doug stretched his long legs over their blanket and set his small ice chest on the far corner of the blanket to mark the territory. "If I'm asleep when you come back, just wake me," he teased.

The two girls headed for the outhouse and were joined by

Katie and another girl from their group named Katrina.

"That was a real cute joke, Christy," Katrina said. "Giving the last float a 10, I mean."

"I don't think she meant it as a joke," Katie said. "Christy happens to be the world's most hopeless romantic. You really did think it deserved a 10, didn't you, Christy?"

"Yes, I did," Christy said.

"Well, I kind of liked it a lot, too," Katrina admitted. "But I wasn't about to let all those guys know."

"Why not?" Christy asked. "They're just guys. Some of them are as romantic as we are, if not more so."

"Who?" Katie challenged. "Rick?"

"No, I meant Doug," Christy said as the girls took their place in the long line at the portable rest room.

She lowered her voice as the other three girls tilted their heads in close. "Did you know that Doug is 20 years old, but he's never kissed a girl?" Christy whispered.

"No way!" Katie said.

"It's true," Tracy confirmed. "He says his first kiss is going to be at the altar on his wedding day."

"Is that romantic or what?" Christy asked.

"Can you imagine how special his wife is going to feel?" Katrina asked in wide-eyed wonder. "She'll probably wish she had never kissed another guy."

"I know," Christy said. "I thought the same thing. Kind of made me wish I'd never kissed a guy before."

"Me, too," said Tracy.

"Me, too," said Katrina.

Christy knew Katie had never been kissed, but instead of Katie popping off with one of her usual jokes about not having that problem, she turned slightly away from the rest of the girls.

"Katie?" Christy asked.

Katie didn't look at her. Christy tried to be funny and said, "Don't you have anything to say here, Katie? You're the only one with virgin lips."

"Whatever," Katie mumbled.

The outhouse door opened, and Katie disappeared inside.

"I don't think Katie's as inexperienced as she may have led you to believe," Katrina said softly.

"Of course she is," Christy said. "I know everything about her. She's never had a boyfriend, and the few dates she's been on have been disasters. Glen, the guy at church that she likes, gave her a hug, but that was all."

Katie exited the rest room, and Christy stopped talking and waited for Tracy, who went in next.

Katie didn't look at Christy but instead spoke to Katrina. "I'm going to go back."

Christy felt awful. She obviously had embarrassed Katie in front of these girls Katie barely knew. It didn't quite seem like the honor Christy had meant when she called Katie "virgin lips." She tried to think how she would feel if she had never had a guy interested in her and her best friend had made a crack like that about her in public.

When the three girls returned to the group, Christy wanted to slip over to Katie and tell her she was sorry. It looked impossible, though, to maneuver through the jam of people without making a scene. Katie was tucked back in her spot, leaning against Rick's legs.

Tracy nimbly made her way back to their blanket, blazing a skinny trail for Christy to follow. The people behind them were not happy about letting them through to their front-row seats.

Doug straightened up when they arrived back in their little

nest and said, "You didn't miss anything. A bunch of horses came by, that's all."

The next float finally arrived, pulled by a tow truck. "Let's hear it for the tow truck!" Rick said and started clapping loudly.

Christy noticed that Katie didn't jump right in and join Rick in his antics. She still seemed upset. As several more floats passed by, Christy kept looking over to see if Katie had snapped out of it, but Katie looked deep in thought.

Near the parade's end, Christy saw Rick lean over and say something in Katie's ear. Her bright smile instantly returned, and she playfully slugged him in the arm. She seemed her old self, and Christy felt relieved.

When the group started to pick up its stuff to leave, Christy reminded her friends, "You guys all know about the party at my aunt and uncle's, right?"

Everyone said, "Yes." A few asked for directions, and one girl asked Christy if they should stop to buy any food.

"No," Christy told her. "I'm sure my aunt has enough for an army."

"Your aunt doesn't know how these guys eat, though," the girl said.

"Actually, she has watched Doug in action, so I think she has a fair idea," Christy said, smiling at Doug, who heard her comment.

"Okay," the girl said, linking arms with the guy beside her. "We'll be there. Thanks for inviting us."

"You're coming with me, aren't you?" Doug asked.

"I guess," Christy answered as she looked around for Katie. "Would it be okay if Katie came with us?" Christy was hoping to use the ride back to apologize to Katie for her insensitive comment.

"Sure, if one of you doesn't mind riding in the middle."

"I'll ride in the middle. Let me go ask her."

Christy wove through the mob and touched Katie on the arm. She was standing next to Rick.

"Katie, do you want to come with Doug and me?"

Katie looked at Rick and then back at Christy. "I don't know. I thought I'd go with Rick since the rest of my stuff is in his car and everything."

"Oh."

Rick stepped in and with his half smile said, "You can come with us, if you want. You can have the whole backseat to yourself."

Something about the way Rick said it felt like a slam to Christy. Why did he assume that Katie would be in the front seat and she would be in the back? Why was he stepping in and acting protective of Katie?

"Thanks," Christy said, forcing a smile at both of them. "I think I'll go with Doug so he won't be by himself."

"Okay," Rick said, sticking his lawn chair under his arm and reaching for the ice chest Katie had in her hand. "We'll see you at Bob and Marti's. I remember how to get there."

Since he had on his sunglasses, Christy couldn't read his expression, but he sounded a little too arrogant and not at all like the tender person who had talked to her on the cement-block wall that morning.

"Ready?" Rick asked Katie, and the two of them headed down the street, with Rick carrying almost all their gear.

Katie didn't say a word to Christy or even look at her. She fell in step with Rick and marched down the street with him, her red hair shining in the late morning sun.

Something felt strange. Christy couldn't quite figure out what it was. She picked her way over the trash that people had left behind them and joined Doug and Tracy.

Tracy had found an empty paper bag and was going around picking up trash.

"Come on," Doug said. "They hire people to do that."

"We left such a mess, though. Let me at least pick up the stuff from our group."

Christy joined her, and in minutes the bag was bulging with candy wrappers and empty soda cans.

"I can't believe how sloppy some people are," Tracy said. Looking up, she realized the rest of their group had disappeared, and only the three of them were left.

"Oh, I guess I'm going to need a ride back," Tracy said to Doug. "Looks as if they all thought I had a ride. Good thing you two are still here."

Christy found another empty bag and, after picking up enough trash to feel she had done her good deed for the day, she said, "We'd better go or else everyone is going to arrive before us."

"You're right," Doug said. "We have a hike back to the truck, and the freeway will be jammed. Think you can leave that for the paid professionals, Tracy?"

"Okay, okay. I'm coming. Where's my sleeping bag?"

"Right here," Doug said, showing the tied-up bundle under his arm. He also had an ice chest, beach chair, two blankets, and Christy's jacket.

"Come on, Tarzan," Tracy said with a laugh, "let Christy and me at least carry the blankets."

Doug shared the load and led the girls back to the truck. It must have been at least a mile, and Christy's feet were starting to hurt. Before she could get in, Tracy slid into the tight middle spot and positioned her short legs to the side of the gears on the floor. Christy was about to argue, but Tracy was definitely smaller, and she did fit in that spot better than Christy.

As Doug had predicted, the freeway on-ramp looked like a parking lot, with cars stacked up for as far as they could see. He turned on the radio and settled back, apparently willing to take it all in stride. Tracy put her head back and closed her eyes, admitting that the all-night party was catching up with her.

Christy looked out the window and thought about Rick and Katie being together somewhere in this mess in his red Mustang. They had been together, just the two of them, all night, and Katie hadn't said a word about what it was like.

A couple of college students, a guy and a girl, were in the back of a pickup truck next to them. The girl looked as though she was trying to sleep. Her head rested against the cab window, and her face was tilted up toward the sun.

A red light forced the pickup to stop, and the guy started to tickle the girl mercilessly. The girl flirted right back, smacking the guy in the stomach. Then he wrapped his arms around her and kissed her. The light turned green, and as the truck moved ahead of them, Christy saw the girl lay her head on the guy's shoulder as if settling back down for a nap.

It reminded Christy of the way Katie had planted herself in front of Rick's chair and had playfully punched him a couple of times during the parade. Suddenly, Christy knew why Katie hadn't admitted to never being kissed.

"Oh no, Katie! You didn't!" Christy spouted.

"What?" Tracy said, jerking forward out of her sleepy state. "What's wrong?"

"Nothing," Christy said. "I'm sorry I woke you. I didn't mean to say anything. I just thought of something, that's all."

Tracy went back to sleep, and Doug tapped his fingers on the steering wheel in time to the song on the radio.

Christy silently shouted to herself, *Katie, tell me you didn't kiss him!*

CHAPTER THIRTEEN

Marti's Party

"Welcome, welcome!" Bob greeted Christy, Doug, and Tracy at the front door nearly two hours later. "Looks as though most of your friends beat you here. Did you have any problems?"

"I stopped for gas," Doug explained, "and then an accident on the freeway held us up. I guess everyone else made it through that stretch before the accident."

"There you are!" Marti said, appearing in the entryway. "Fourteen, 15, 16," she pointed her finger at each of them as she counted. "We now have 16 guests. You said you were expecting 17, Christy."

"I think everyone is probably here, Aunt Marti," answered Christy. "What about my parents and David? Are they here yet?"

"No," Marti explained, "they decided not to come. I told your mom about our big party, and she decided it might be best if they sat this one out. I told her you could ride back to Escondido with Rick."

Oh, great! That's just what I need, a view from Rick's backseat of this budding romance between him and Katie.

"By the way," Marti said, taking Christy by the arm and leading her into the family room, which was crowded with all her guests, "who is that redheaded girl who arrived with Rick? Are they dating now? They make a stunning couple."

"That's my best friend, Katie," Christy said, pulling her arm from Marti's grip and getting out of the noisy family room as quickly as she could.

She retreated to the kitchen. Heather was the only other person there; she was stacking two hefty sandwiches onto a plate. The selection and amount of sandwich preparations Marti had laid out on the counter was mammoth. It looked like enough food for 117 people.

"I don't know why I let those guys talk me into making these sandwiches for them. It's their seconds, not mine. Who do they think I am? Their personal slave?" Heather said.

"Then send them in here to make their sandwiches themselves," Christy advised.

Heather giggled, her wispy, blonde hair falling over her eyes. "I don't really mind. It's kind of fun, actually. Besides, if I want to be great in God's kingdom, I'm supposed to be the servant of all, right?"

Christy grabbed a soda from the ice chest and said, "Yeah, well, as long as the guys know that verse applies to them, too. They're supposed to serve us right back!"

"Good point," Heather said, carefully balancing the loaded paper plate and heading out the door. "I think I'll bring that point up at halftime."

Christy went over to the sink, filled a glass halfway, and popped Rick's white rose into the water. Placing it in the center of the kitchen table, she slid into a chair and nibbled on a potato chip from one of the six assorted bags before her.

She thought about Heather's servanthood quip and remembered Doug saying people are supposed to be servants of God and not treat Him as though He were their personal slave. Doug also said the key was in surrendering.

"Okay, God," she prayed softly in the empty kitchen, "I surrender, again. Here I thought something might happen between Doug and me, but he sees me as his little sister. And then I thought I could patch things up with Rick and feel good about everything with him, but now I'm all upset that he likes Katie. I give up! I can't make things work out the way I want them to. I surrender all these guys in my life to You."

Just then Heather slipped back in and with a giggle said, "Oops! I forgot to get myself something to drink."

She scooped a soft drink from the ice chest and held it up in a good-bye gesture on her way back to the family room. She was almost through the door when she stopped, turned around, and looked at Christy.

"Are you okay?" she cautiously asked.

"Sure. Why?"

Heather sat down across the table from Christy. "Oh, no reason. Except that this is your party, and everyone is in the other room, but you're sitting here all by yourself."

"I had some thinking to do," Christy answered.

"About Rick and Katie and what's up with them?" Heather ventured, opening her can and taking a sip.

Christy smiled at her friend. "How did you know?"

"An educated guess," Heather said with a grin. "The last time I saw you with Rick you were trying to talk yourself into being glad you were going together. Then I saw him last week sledding with Katie and figured out real fast that some strange competitive thing was going on between them."

"Sounds about right," Christy said with a sigh.

"Then at pizza that night, it didn't exactly take a rocket

scientist to figure out that you had broken up with him, he was ticked, and he was using all his immature stunts to get your attention." Heather took another sip and said, "You know, to be honest, I thought for sure that night when you two left together you were going to kiss and make up and get back together."

Christy smirked. "The exact opposite happened. I pushed Rick even further away. I didn't mean to. It just turned out that way."

"I think that means that deep down you wanted to send him away. You wanted to be done with your relationship with him," Heather said, looking at Christy for agreement.

"Oh, come on, Heather! You said the same thing when I agreed to go steady with Rick. Remember, in the bathroom at Tracy's house, when I was crying because I wasn't sure I'd done the right thing? You said I agreed to go steady with him because deep down I really wanted to."

"Well? Didn't you?"

"I don't know anymore. I wish I'd never gone out with him."

They paused while another girl slipped in and out of the kitchen, grabbing two sodas.

"Look," Heather said calmly, "I may not always be the best advice-giver, but I know that you need to forget the past and press on toward the future. That's not my stupid advice. It's in the Bible, so I know it's true."

Christy remembered reading that verse before. It was in Philippians. She'd read the short book of Philippians more than any other book in the Bible, except maybe for some of the psalms.

"You're right," Christy told Heather. "I need to look forward. After all, this is the beginning of a new year, right?"

"Right!" Heather said. "And if there is something going on between Rick and Katie, maybe the best thing to do is let it run its natural course. You don't know. They might really be good for each other. They say opposites attract."

"So I've heard," Christy said. "You're right, Heather. When I started going out with Rick, Katie was supportive of me. She didn't really agree with my dating him, and every now and then she'd let me know her opinion. Still, she never stopped treating me like her best friend. I think it might be my turn to be a servant and treat her like my best friend, even though I'm not crazy about her going out with Rick."

"And you can tell her that honestly," Heather added. "Katie didn't hide her opinion of Rick while you were dating him. Tell Katie honestly what you think."

"Okay. I will. Thanks, Heather. You always seem to pop up at the right time. I really appreciate you."

Heather smiled. "Good! Because that's my New Year's resolution—to learn to be the servant of all. I'm glad to have been of service."

Christy felt relieved and almost ready to face the mob in the other room when the kitchen door swung halfway open and the back of Katie's red head appeared.

"And Speed," Rick's voice boomed over the clamor in the other room, "don't forget the mustard this time!"

"Yes, Master," Katie responded, playfully bowing from the waist. She spun around with a huge grin, which vanished when she spotted Christy.

The two friends locked gazes.

Heather slipped from her seat and said, "You know, Katie, I was just going to make myself a sandwich. Can I make that one for Rick, and you can do something else? Like, say, maybe take my place at the table and help Christy guard all those potato chips?"

"Turkey with everything, including mustard," Katie said, handing the empty plate to Heather. Her eyes still fixed on Christy, Katie headed for the table and said, "I already know what you're going to say."

"No, you don't."

"Yes, I do."

"No, you don't!" Christy said firmly. "You don't know what I'm going to say."

"Okay," Katie said. "Fine. What would you like to say to me?"

"First, I want to apologize. My crack about 'virgin lips' at the parade was stupid, and I'm sorry I said it."

Katie looked away.

"Will you please forgive me?" Christy asked.

"Sure," Katie said, still not looking at Christy. "Don't worry about it."

"There's more," Christy said. "You're my best friend, Katie. We have to stick together."

Heather left with a plate of sandwiches; in the crook of her elbow were two sodas. She gave Christy a "thumbs up" sign as she disappeared.

Christy thought she saw a tear fall from Katie's eye onto her lap.

Christy continued. "If you like Rick, that's fine with me. Really. I talked with him this morning, and I feel as though things are settled between us. We're just friends. He can be interested in whomever he wants to be interested in. And if that's you, then that's great!"

Katie looked up. There were tears in her eyes. "You really mean that?"

"Yes, I really mean that. It's hard because I don't want you to get your feelings hurt by Rick the way I did. But you and I are different in a lot of ways, and you might be good for him. And he might be good for you. I don't know. I don't want to come between you two. Your friendship means more to me than that."

Katie pressed her lips together and looked as though she might be swallowing hard to keep from crying. In a cracked voice, she said, "He kissed me, Christy."

"I know," Christy answered softly.

Katie's green eyes suddenly flared up. "How did you know? Did he tell you? That jerk!"

"No, Rick didn't tell me. I just knew. I know you, Katie, and I could tell. Not at first, but I figured it out."

"It wasn't like you think," Katie began. "I didn't know he was going to do it. It was New Year's, you know. Everyone on the street was having this big party, and at midnight we all counted down, and then all of a sudden Rick kissed me. Everyone was kissing. It was New Year's!"

"Katie, I know. You don't have to explain anything to me. It's fine!"

"But it's not fine! He came at me so fast and strong, I didn't know how to respond. And the worst part is, you were right about the virgin lips, up until last night. I'd never been kissed. And Christy, I've been so jealous of you! I never thought any guy would want to kiss me, least of all someone like Rick."

Christy reached for a napkin on the counter and handed it to Katie to blot her eyes. "You deserve the best guy in the world, Katie."

"Do you know how awful it feels to be kissed for the very first time and think you can't ever, ever tell your best friend?"

"I'm sure my 'virgin lips' comment didn't help."

"It wasn't even that. It was the horrible, mixed-up feelings of wanting to feel so special, because in my wildest dreams I never pictured a guy like Rick ever kissing me, and then he does. And then I felt awful."

"Don't feel awful," Christy said. "Try to see it for what it was. It was your first kiss, and that's a very wonderful thing. It was New Year's, and there's nothing wrong with a quick little kiss at midnight." Christy scanned Katie's face for the truth as she delicately asked, "That's all it was, wasn't it? One little kiss? I mean, you guys didn't sit and make out all night or anything."

"Of course not!" Katie looked offended. "We sat up all night and played cards with the people next to us and told stupid elephant jokes. It was the most fun New Year's I've ever had."

"Then there's no reason to feel bad."

"I didn't until you guys started saying all that stuff about Doug never kissing a girl," Katie said. "But then I think he's a little extreme. I mean, isn't there someplace in the middle where you can kiss every now and then, and it doesn't mean you're a loose woman?"

"I'm not sure. I guess so," Christy said. "I admire Doug, though. I think he's going to make his wife feel so special."

"Yeah, on their wedding day she'll feel really special," Katie said. "But I would imagine she'll feel like dog meat all the months they date and during their engagement if he never kisses her. I mean, I don't think there's anything wrong with light kissing to show your affection. It's all the other stuff that I think should be saved for marriage."

"I agree. And you could be right about Doug being a little extreme. For someone like Doug who's such a natural hugger, it does seem he would be a little freer with his kisses. Still, I admire him because he's made a decision and stuck to it. Plus, it seems he and Tracy didn't have much trouble switching from dating to friends, because they didn't have any of that physical stuff to try to erase from their relationship."

Katie reached for a potato chip, obviously feeling better. "I admire that," Katie admitted. "I also admire you and Todd, and I don't see how his kissing you a few times made it any easier or harder when he left for Hawaii. That guy is in your heart. I think you'd feel the same way about him even if he'd never kissed you."

"You could be right," Christy said with a sigh.

"Of course I'm right!" Katie said, picking up steam. "If you want to know my opinion, you should take your own advice, Christy, and hold out for a hero, no matter what the state of his lips—virgin or not."

Christy laughed and said, "Okay, I will, as long as you take the same advice, and you hold out for a hero, too. I'm not saying that Rick isn't that hero. He could be. I don't know. But promise me you'll settle for nothing but the best."

Katie's bright smile returned, flashing her agreement and making Christy feel much better.

Remembering her earlier prayer of surrender, Christy thought, *This servant stuff might not be so hard after all. God sure has a way of working everything out when I let Him.*

"Shall we join the party?" Christy asked Katie just as an unusually loud roar rose in the family room.

"Must be a major touchdown," Katie said, grabbing a bag of chips and fishing for a can of soda in the ice chest.

"Listen," Christy said, "that's Marti screaming. She's not much of a football fan. And that sounds like Tracy shouting. They must be having a pillow fight in there."

"Come on!" Katie urged, grabbing a slice of cheese and sticking it in her mouth. "Grab the M&M's and let's show those guys a real pillow fight!"

Christy grabbed the jumbo bag of M&M's. Just as they were about to exit the kitchen, the door swung open. Uncle Bob stood before them, his face red with excitement. Around his neck he wore a Hawaiian lei made from plumeria that were no longer white but looked brown and travel-worn.

"I think you'd better come out here, Christy," Bob said. "It appears guest number 17 has just arrived."

CHAPTER FOURTEEN

Counting Stars

"Todd!" Christy screamed, throwing the bag of M&M's into the air and racing past her uncle into the family room. There, encircled by his shocked friends, stood a tanned, sun-bleached-blond Todd. Around his neck hung half a dozen crushed leis.

"Todd!" Christy called out again, sprinting across the room. The group of friends stood back, making way for Christy.

When Todd heard her calling his name, he pulled away from Heather's hug around his neck and looked for Christy. Those silver-blue eyes that Christy had dreamed about met her gaze across the room. Todd's face lit up, and he opened his arms to receive her embrace.

Just before Christy reached him, she spotted a white sling on his left arm. With great self-control, she curbed her hug to a modified side squeeze on his right side.

"What happened?" she breathed into his ear, her tears giving way and trickling down his T-shirt.

"It's nothing. Here," he said as she pulled back. "This is for you, *Kilikina*."

Feeling the warmth of hearing him call her his special Hawaiian version of her name, Christy watched as Todd looped a

135

plumeria and orchid lei off his neck and placed it around her neck, kissing her once on each cheek.

"Aloha, *Kilikina*," he said softly.

The tropical fragrance of the plumeria set off a cascade of hopes, joys, and dreams in her heart. "You're back" was all she could say.

Todd's gaze left her face and locked on the gold bracelet circling her right wrist. A huge grin spread across his face. He kissed Christy again on her damp cheeks and said, "Yes, I'm back."

"Well? Tell us what happened!" Marti said, eagerly wedging her way into the circle. "Are you through with surfing for a while?"

"Looks like it," Todd said, raising his sling for emphasis. "Here, Marti. You need one of these."

He began to remove one of his leis for her when Marti protested. "Oh, no, give them to the younger girls first. Look, Katie doesn't have one yet."

Katie shyly stepped forward, and Todd presented her with a lei, kissing her on the cheek in the Hawaiian custom. Christy thought it looked as if Katie were blushing. Oddly, Christy didn't feel jealous. She knew Todd's kisses on her cheek, even in front of everyone, were different from what the others received.

The football game was forgotten as everyone started to ask Todd questions.

"Whoa!" Bob said. "Let's let the poor guy catch his breath. Are you hungry, Todd? Come into the kitchen and get yourself something to eat."

The group followed Todd into the kitchen, and he answered questions along the way.

"I arrived this afternoon—an hour ago. Doug's mom said you were all over here. I was on standby out of Honolulu, and they had an opening on a flight early this morning."

Marti handed him a soda as Bob spread some mayonnaise on a French roll. "What do you think, Todd? A little of everything?"

"Sure, that would be great," he said, sitting at the table, popping open his soda, and taking a long drink.

"What happened with the surfing?" Doug asked, joining the others crowded around the table.

Christy had managed to slide in and take the empty chair next to Todd. She scooted closer to him so Tracy could wedge in next to her. That made room for Rick to slip a bar stool in on the end.

"Surfing was outrageous," Todd said, a smile lighting up his tanned face.

His skin was so dark. Even in the summer Christy had never seen him this bronzed. And his hair looked almost white. She noticed it was a lot longer than she had ever seen it, especially in the back, where it curled on the nape of his neck. Todd looked different—really good, but different.

"The championships," Doug said, bringing Todd back from his apparent daydream of the foaming waves. "What happened? Did you drop out?"

"Sort of," Todd said, chomping into the huge sandwich Bob placed before him.

Everyone waited while Todd chewed and swallowed.

"Great sandwich," he said to Bob. "*Mahalo.*"

Come on, you surfed-out beach boy! Christy thought. *Stop being so easygoing and tell us what happened.*

"The big ones came in at Waimea last Monday afternoon," Todd began, gulping his soda. "Man, you can't imagine the feeling of standing on a beach you've stood on day after day and looking at an ocean you only played in before. All of a sudden everything is changed. The waves are so outrageous. When they crash on the sand, you can feel it through the bottoms of your feet."

The group bent in closer. Todd took another bite, smiling at each of them with his eyes.

"Nobody went out right away. You have to get psyched up for waves like that. You know it's going to be a wrangle between you and the wave. Only one of you is going to win. You have to make sure it's going to be you before you go out there."

"Is that how you hurt your arm?" Heather asked.

Todd took another bite and another swig of soda. Instead of answering her, he continued the story. "Kimo was ready first. I think Kimo was born ready."

"Now, who is Kimo?" Marti asked.

"The guy I went to school with when I grew up on Maui," Todd answered and took another bite.

Christy filled in for him while he ate. "Todd stayed with Kimo over there. The two of them always wanted to get on the pro surfing circuit, ever since they were kids. Kimo has a house on the North Shore of Oahu."

"More like a shack," Todd said with a laugh. "A lot of times we just slept on the beach, his apartment was so full of cockroaches, centipedes, and geckos. It was hard to sleep at night with all the local critters crawling across my face."

Christy could easily believe Todd had spent the last few months sleeping on the beach and living off the land. He certainly looked like an island boy. Knowing him as she did, she imagined such a life must have been a dream come true for him.

"So Kimo takes this wave on, and he makes it!" Todd's eyes grew wide. "I mean, this is like riding down the side of a four-story building, and he makes it look like nothing. Now we're all psyched. If Kimo can take it, we all want a ride."

"Was this part of the competition?" Tracy asked.

"No, competition wasn't supposed to start until the next day. The waves showed up early. We all paddled out, feeling the spray on our faces. There it is, man! This monstrous wall of pure blue, and we all know it's the day of reckoning."

Christy remembered the cover on the surfing magazine with the huge wave, shooting the surfboards to shore like toy arrows. She also remembered that it was a Monday. Todd said they were surfing the big waves on a Monday. *I wonder if the Monday I prayed for Todd at work was the same Monday he's talking about?*

"Eddie catches it on the outside," Todd continued, "and in seconds he's shot out of the water like a rocket, with his board right behind him. Before I even have a chance to feel the fear, it's my turn, and all of a sudden, I'm on it. I'm riding this monster to shore! I'm riding it!"

"Weren't you afraid that you were going to be killed?" Marti asked. "Didn't you think of that, Todd?"

Todd smiled and said, "Actually, I thought of Elijah."

"Elijah?" Marti asked. "Who's that? One of your surfing friends?"

"No, you know, Elijah, the great man of God in the book of First Kings. Remember? He stood in a cave on the side of a mountain waiting for the presence of the Lord to pass by. First a wind came that tore the mountain apart, then an earthquake, then a fire. But God's presence wasn't in those natural things. Finally, Elijah heard a gentle whisper, and he knew that was God's voice speaking to him."

Marti blinked and glanced around at the group of teens nodding their understanding. Obviously, Marti had never heard that Bible story before.

"That's what I felt like," Todd said. "There I was, standing in the hollow of this mountain of a wave, everything crashing around me and then right here," he said, patting his chest, "I felt this total calm, and I knew God was about to do something."

Everyone remained still, waiting for Todd to continue. His expression looked a little glazed as he said, "That's when I saw Kimo's board shooting past me, and I couldn't see Kimo anywhere. So I plant my feet, and I ride this killer wave. It felt like Jell-O under my board. I could bend and turn that wave any way I wanted to, and it carried me like a baby in a basket. I rode it all the way to shore, man! Do you know what I'm saying? A wave like that only comes once in a surfer's life. This was my wave!"

"What happened to the other guys?" Tracy asked.

"When I hit the sand, an ambulance was there, and two lifeguards were pulling Eddie out of the water. They started CPR, and I started to pray and scan the water for Kimo."

"Oh, how awful!" Marti spoke up. "Why did you boys ever do such a foolish thing? You could have all been killed!"

"I'm not afraid of anything in creation," Todd answered. "I know the Creator."

"What happened to Kimo and Eddie?" Christy asked. "Were they all right?"

"Kimo came up spewing chunks, and Eddie came real close to going to hell," Todd said bluntly.

One of his grins spread across his face, and he said, "Then they both got saved, right there on the beach!"

Christy and most of the others knew what Todd meant and expressed their joy and amazement. Marti, however, looked to Bob for an explanation. Bob only shrugged his shoulders.

"The paramedics were able to revive them, you mean?" Marti said.

"Oh, yeah, their lives were spared, and I'm sure the paramedics helped out with that. But they both surrendered their lives to

God, right there on the beach, with the waves spraying them and a whole crowd of people watching. It was the most incredible thing I've ever seen!"

"These guys you were staying with this whole time weren't Christians?" Doug asked.

"Not when I got there. That's mostly what I did for the last four months—tell them about Jesus. When I left yesterday, five of them had laid down their weapons and surrendered to God. It was like a revival, man!"

Marti looked perturbed, and in an effort to change the subject, said, "You still haven't told us about the competition. How did your tryouts go? That's what you worked so hard for, wasn't it?"

"I didn't go," Todd said, munching on his last bite of sandwich.

"What?"

"Hey, I surfed *my* wave on Monday. I'll never surf another wave like that—ever. Kimo got saved. That's what I went for."

"I don't understand," Marti said, looking to Bob for interpretation.

"What about your arm?" Bob asked, motioning to the sling. Todd held it up and said, "Centipede. I got bit last week and ended up in the hospital. Seems I'm more allergic to centipedes than I am to bees."

Christy jumped in and told everyone how Todd was stung by a bee last summer on his foot and how it swelled up twice its size. "He has to carry around this kit to give himself an injection or else he stops breathing."

"Now I have two kits," Todd joked. "A bee antigen kit and a centipede kit."

"We're all glad you're back and in one piece," Tracy said.

"Think you'll stay around for a while?"

"I have to get into school somewhere."

"Where do you want to go?" Doug asked.

"Any place where I can transfer my credits from the University of Hawaii."

"That shouldn't be too hard to find," Doug said. "Have you considered the ever-popular San Diego State?"

"As a matter of fact, I have," Todd said.

"It just so happens Rick and I lost our roommate at the end of last semester. We're looking for somebody to start paying rent on that empty room. What do you think, Rick? Did we just find our third amigo?"

Christy couldn't believe this was happening. It was freaky enough when Rick moved in with Doug last fall. But the thought of the three of them sharing the same apartment was too much.

Rick sounded casual when he answered, "Sure. He looks harmless enough. But can he cook? Or do we feed him bananas and coconuts off the tree?"

Christy wondered if this living arrangement would really work. Could Rick see Todd as anything but a competitor? Time would tell.

The group around the table started to break up. The guys headed back to the family room to see what had happened in the game. And Doug and most of the girls stuck around to ask Todd questions about Hawaii and what it was like to go to college there.

Christy had felt her stomach grumbling for the last half hour and thought it was the excitement over Todd. But with a glance at the clock, she realized it was dinnertime. All she had eaten since the muffins in Doug's truck that morning were a few potato chips.

As she folded the thin slices of roast beef onto her piece of bread, Christy caught Todd looking at her while still answering questions. She pointed at the food and mouthed the words, "Do you want another?" Todd nodded, and she eagerly set to work making him a masterpiece. It felt so good to have him back.

But Christy really felt like a princess when everyone started to leave. She had already asked Katie and Rick if she could catch a ride home with them, and Rick had agreed nicely, without making any comment about her sitting in the backseat.

Todd came up beside her and asked, "Would it be okay if I drove you home?"

She was about to protest that it was a long drive and he must be tired, but no words formed on her lips. She only smiled at him and nodded her appreciation.

Once they had said good-bye to everyone, gathered Christy's things, and thanked Bob and Marti several times, Todd and Christy stepped into the cool January night. He led her half a block down the street to where he had parked his Volkswagen van, "Gus the Bus."

He opened the side door and tossed Christy's suitcase inside. Even the door's sound filled her with memories.

She recalled the first time she had ridden in Gus. Thinking Todd had asked her for a date, she had dressed up. But he had arrived with Gus loaded with people all casually dressed, and off they went to a concert at his church.

Now Todd opened her door, and this time she climbed into an empty but musty-smelling van and adjusted her position so she wouldn't sit on the rip that had begun in the seat.

"Smells like Gus needs a bath," Christy said when Todd got in.

"He's been locked in my dad's garage since I left." Todd started up the engine and drove a few blocks, sniffing the air. "Oh,

I think I know what it is," he said, pulling into a gas station and jumping out.

He pulled out a pizza box from under the driver's seat and gingerly lifted the lid with his bandaged arm.

"If that's what I think it is," Christy said, eyeing the box Todd had snapped shut, "I don't want to know how long it's been under there, and I don't want to know what color the fungus is."

Todd jogged over to a trash can and dumped the moldy pizza.

Returning, he said, "It's kind of a shame to waste a perfectly good science experiment like that. Your little brother could have gotten an A with that one."

"Todd, do you know how gross that is?"

He laughed and said, "You should have looked at it, Christy. You really missed a miracle of nature!"

"I can think of other miracles of nature that I prefer over a five-month-old piece of pizza."

They talked and laughed for the first half hour of their drive down the coast. Somewhere near San Clemente, Todd pulled off the main highway and drove on a bumpy dirt road up the side of a deserted hill. City lights were behind them, but the farther up Todd drove, the darker it became. He coaxed Gus over several huge ruts in the road. Suddenly, the road leveled out, and they were on a flat surface.

"Where are we?" Christy asked.

"You can't see it in the dark, but that's Tressels down there."

"Tressels?"

"Surfing spot," Todd explained. "It's a good one."

This is it? You risked my life to bring me up this road to show me a surfing spot I can't even see in the dark?

"Come on," Todd said, reaching for Christy's jacket in the backseat. "I want to show you something."

Christy got out carefully, unable to see if she was about to step on firm footing or fall off a cliff.

"What way did you go, Todd? I can't see anything."

"I'm up here," he called, and she looked around to see how his voice could suddenly be coming from above her. "I'm on top of Gus. Come around to the back, and I'll give you a hand up." Christy felt her way along Gus's side. Once she reached the back, she placed her foot on the bumper.

"There's a little thing to put your foot on," Todd instructed. "Good, you've got it. Now give me your hand." He helped her up, and Christy, still unsure of herself, crawled over to where he had spread out her jacket. She sat down and waited for Todd to join her.

He sat down close beside her and said nothing. Christy remembered when they had sat nearly this close on the beach several months ago. It was the morning Todd had announced he was going to Hawaii. He had told her he was selfish to try to hold on to her and wait for her to grow up. And then he put his hand on her forehead and blessed her.

That was a horrible morning. It was basically where they had left off.

Tonight, just like that morning, Todd said nothing. He stared at the stars.

In the past, such silences had made Christy nervous, wondering what he was thinking, wondering if she should say something.

Now she didn't mind the stillness. Todd was here, beside her. They could be together and be silent. The main thing was that they were together.

Christy tilted her head back and looked at the stars.

"Last time I watched the heavens like this was on Christmas Eve," Todd said.

"Really? Me, too! We were in the mountains on Christmas Eve, and I sat for a long time and looked at the stars out my bedroom window," Christy told him.

"Imagine," Todd said, "we were looking at the same stars the same night except I was sitting on a beach 5,000 miles away. What were you thinking about that night?"

Christy wished she could tell Todd that she had been thinking about him and dreaming about when he would come back. She couldn't lie, so she told him, "I was thinking about Jesus, when He was a baby. I was wondering if He noticed the bright Bethlehem star from His manger."

"Do you know what I was thinking about?" Todd asked. Without waiting for her to answer, he continued. "I was thinking of Abraham."

Christy wished he had said he was thinking about her. Still, why should she be surprised that Todd would think of something spiritual and bizarre on Christmas Eve? *After all, I was thinking about Jesus watching stars from His manger. Oh no, maybe I'm starting to think of everything in spiritual terms like Todd!*

"Remember how God made him a promise?" Todd interrupted her thoughts.

"Wasn't he supposed to become the father of a great nation?" Christy asked.

"Right. Father of a great nation—a guy who had no kids. It seemed like a big joke. Then God told him to step outside his tent one night and said, 'Look up in the heavens, Abe. Count the stars if you can. That's how many descendants you're going to have.'"

"I remember that story," Christy said.

"Well, did you know that after God made that promise, He turned silent? God didn't speak to Abraham again for years and years."

She had always enjoyed Todd's insights into God, and tonight they seemed even more wonderful with the sky above them ablaze with the very same stars God had pointed out to Abraham that holy night thousands of years ago.

"Don't you see?" Todd said. "God made one promise, and He disappeared. Can you imagine how Abraham felt year after year? He had no kids, he had no proof God had ever talked to him. All he had was a bunch of silent stars up in the sky to keep counting and keep believing that God really did make him a promise."

"That takes a lot of faith," Christy said.

"I want to have faith like that," Todd said, turning to Christy.

His voice became low and serious. "I don't know exactly what it is God has promised me about you, about us, and about what the future holds."

Christy could feel her heart pound faster. She had waited two years for Todd to verbalize some kind of commitment to her. Could this be it?

"I believe God has planned for us to be friends—close friends. I promised you I'd be your friend forever, *Kilikina*. I want to have faith like Abraham that whatever that means to God, that He'll work it out for us in His time. I want to keep listening for God's voice."

Then, slipping his arm around Christy and drawing her close, Todd said, "For now I guess we keep counting stars."

Christy snuggled her head on Todd's shoulder and whispered softly into the starry night, "Then this is where I want to be. Right beside you, forever counting stars."

Don't Miss These Captivating Stories in
THE CHRISTY MILLER SERIES

#1 • Summer Promise
Christy spends the summer at the beach with her wealthy aunt and uncle. Will she do something she'll later regret?

#2 • A Whisper and a Wish
Christy is convinced that dreams do come true when her family moves to California and the cutest guy in school shows an interest in her.

#3 • Yours Forever
Fifteen-year-old Christy does everything in her power to win Todd's attention.

#4 • Surprise Endings
Christy tries out for cheerleader, learns a classmate is out to get her, and schedules two dates for the same night.

#5 • Island Dreamer
It's an incredible tropical adventure when Christy celebrates her 16th birthday on Maui.

#6 • A Heart Full of Hope
A dazzling dream date, a wonderful job, a great car. And lots of freedom! Christy has it all. Or does she?

#7 • True Friends
Christy sets out with the ski club and discovers the group is thinking of doing something more than hitting the slopes.

#8 • Starry Night
Christy is torn between going to the Rose Bowl Parade with her friends or on a surprise vacation with her family.

#9 • Seventeen Wishes
Christy is off to summer camp—as a counselor for a cabin of wild fifth-grade girls.

#10 • A Time to Cherish
A surprise houseboat trip! Her senior year! Lots of friends! Life couldn't be better for Christy until . . .

#11 • Sweet Dreams
Christy's dreams become reality when Todd finally opens his heart to her. But her relationship with her best friend goes downhill fast when Katie starts dating Michael, and Christy has doubts about their relationship.

#12 • A Promise Is Forever
On a European trip with her friends, Christy finds it difficult to keep her mind off Todd. Will God bring them back together?

9803

THE SIERRA JENSEN SERIES

If you've enjoyed reading about Christy Miller,
you'll love reading about Christy's friend Sierra Jensen.

#1 • Only You, Sierra
When her family moves to another state, Sierra dreads going to a new high school—until she meets Paul.

#2 • In Your Dreams
Just when events in Sierra's life start to look up—she even gets asked out on a date—Sierra runs into Paul.

#3 • Don't You Wish
Sierra is excited about visiting Christy Miller in California during Easter break. Unfortunately, her sister, Tawni, decides to go with her.

#4 • Close Your Eyes
Sierra experiences a sticky situation when Paul comes over for dinner and Randy shows up at the same time.

#5 • Without A Doubt
When handsome Drake reveals his interest in Sierra, life gets complicated.

#6 • With This Ring
Sierra couldn't be happier when she goes to Southern California to join Christy Miller and their friends for Doug and Tracy's wedding.

#7 • Open Your Heart
When Sierra's friend Christy Miller receives a scholarship from a university in Switzerland, she invites Sierra to go with her and Aunt Marti to visit the school.

#8 • Time Will Tell
After an exciting summer in Southern California and Switzerland, Sierra returns home to several unsettled relationships.

#9 • Now Picture This
When Sierra and Paul start corresponding, she imagines him as her boyfriend and soon begins neglecting her family and friends.

#10 • Hold On Tight
Sierra joins her brother and several friends on a road trip to Southern California to visit potential colleges.

#11 • Closer Than Ever
When Paul doesn't show up for her graduation party and news comes that a flight from London has crashed, Sierra frantically worries about the future.

#12 • Take My Hand
A costly misunderstanding leaves Sierra anxious as she says goodbye to Portland and heads off to California for her freshman year of college.

FOCUS ON THE FAMILY®
LIKE THIS BOOK?

Then you'll love *Brio* magazine! Written especially for teen girls, it's packed each month with 32 pages on everything from fiction and faith to fashion, food . . . even guys! Best of all, it's all from a Christian perspective! But don't just take our word for it. Instead, see for yourself by requesting a complimentary copy.

Simply write Focus on the Family, Colorado Springs, CO 80995 (in Canada, write P.O. Box 9800, Stn. Terminal, Vancouver, B.C. V6B 4G3) and mention that you saw this offer in the back of this book. You may also call 1-800-232-6459 (in Canada, call 1-800-661-9800).

You may also visit our Web site (www.family.org) to learn more about the ministry or find out if there is a Focus on the Family office in your country.

— — —

Want to become everyone's favorite baby-sitter? Then *The Ultimate Baby-Sitter's Survival Guide* is for you! It's packed with page after page of practical information and ways to stay in control; organize mealtime, bath time and bedtime; and handle emergency situations. It also features an entire section of safe, creative and downright crazy indoor and outdoor activities that will keep kids challenged, entertained and away from the television. Easy-to-read and reference, it's the ideal book for providing the best care to children, earning money and having fun at the same time.

Call Focus on the Family at the number above, or check out your local Christian bookstore.

Focus on the Family is an organization that is dedicated to helping you and your family establish lasting, loving relationships with each other and the Lord. It's why we exist! If we can assist you or your family in any way, please feel free to contact us. We'd love to hear from you!